LOVE'S SERENADE

DECADES:
A JOURNEY OF AFRICAN AMERICAN ROMANCE

January	February	March
A DELICATE AFFAIR — LINDSAY EVANS	Secret Desire — KAIA DANIELLE	LOVE'S SERENADE — SHERYL LISTER

April	May	June
THE ART OF LOVE — SUZETTE D. HARRISON	LOVE'S SWEET Melody — KIANNA ALEXANDER	PRIDE & PASSION — CARLA BUCHANAN

July	August	September
PROMISE ME A DREAM — WAYNE JORDAN	ELECTION Day — KEITH THOMAS WALKER	MADE TO HOLD YOU — LELE WRIGHT

October	November	December
THUG Love — ZURI DAY	INCONSEQUENTIAL CONSEQUENCES — DENISE JEFFRIES	CAMPAIGN FOR HER Heart — PATRICIA SARGEANT

LOVE'S SERENADE

Decades: A Journey of African American Romance

Sheryl Lister

PROLOGUE

Magnolia, Arkansas
June, 1924

"Hurry up, Mae Lee. Your parents will be back soon."

Mary Lee Johnson turned slightly. "Miles Cooper, I told you to stop calling me that old country name." Miles gave her the patented grin that had melted her the first time she'd seen him playing the piano in Mr. Butler's basement saloon.

Miles chuckled. "Then what should I call you?"

"Leigh. Leigh Jones. When I get to New York, that's who I'll be."

He placed a quick kiss on her lips and picked up her suitcase. "You won't be going anywhere if we don't hurry up and get out of here." He paused. "Are you sure this is what you want to do?"

"Yes. I want to sing and this will be the best chance for me to follow my dreams. I've devoted my whole life trying to please my parents. Just recently, they offered my services to carry food baskets to the sick and shut in, never mind all the other chores I have to do. I kept my mouth shut because that's how I was raised—to obey my parents." She rubbed a weary hand across her forehead. "It seems my entire world revolves around volunteering on every church committee and spending my evenings and summers taking lessons to students who missed school."

He stroked a finger down her cheek. "That's because you have a big heart."

"I don't know about all that, but for once, I want to do something for me. Something that makes *me* happy." Besides, she had no desire to stay and marry Percy. Percival Williams, the pastor's nephew, had somehow convinced her parents that he would make her a good husband and her father had promised her hand to him three weeks ago. But the man masquerading as a minister was fifteen years her senior, a weasel and a thief. Mary hated him. She snatched up her handbag and placed the note she'd written to her parents on the bed. After taking one last glance around, she turned off the lamp and headed out the back door. They made their way through the thick stand of trees at the rear of the property and exited to the road a half a mile away, where a car sat waiting.

The driver hopped out, helped them load the bags and quickly pulled away. He let them out at the boarding house where Miles stayed and would be back at sunrise to drive them to the train station in Louisiana.

Mary followed Miles inside to his room. She took in the sparse furnishings. "There isn't much here." The front room held a chair, table and lamp.

Miles shrugged. "I don't need much." He led her to the bedroom and set the bag down. "You want something to eat or drink?"

"No, thank you. We have a long day tomorrow. I think I just want to turn in." She wondered if he planned for them to sleep together. Though she loved him and had given him her innocence, she wasn't sure about the arrangement.

He must have sensed her hesitancy because he said, "I can sleep on the floor if you're uncomfortable."

"No, no. I'm fine." She grabbed her nightclothes and went into the bathroom to change. When she came out, he was in bed, his bare chest visible above the sheet. Mary laid her dress over the chair and climbed in next to him.

He turned off the light, pulled her close and draped an arm around her waist. "Good night, Leigh."

Smiling, she closed her eyes. A heartbeat later, she was asleep.

Mary woke up the next morning alone. "Miles?" No answer. Puzzled, she took care of her needs, dressed and went downstairs to search the dining room. Not finding him, she returned to the room. On the side table, she noticed a piece of paper with her name on it and a stack of bills beneath it. Her eyes widened as she read. She rushed to the bedroom, pulled out the drawers and found them all empty. He was gone. Her gaze strayed to her slightly opened handbag on the chair. "No," she whispered. A quick search confirmed what she already knew. Some of her music sheets were gone, too. A knock at the door startled her. Her ride. Fighting back tears, Mary gathered up her belongings and vowed never to trust anyone again with her music…or her heart.

Chapter 1

Harlem, New York
May, 1927

Leigh Jones dropped down on the side of her bed, kicked off her shoes and sighed in relief. Her feet ached, her head ached and she smelled like a smoke stack. Just as she'd done every Saturday night for the past three years since coming north, she'd spent the evening singing at rent parties and basement speakeasies—some of which no woman should venture inside. She shuddered at the memories. Thankfully, the piano player who accompanied her made sure she'd had no problems. Offers to sing in the big name clubs were few and far between, often times booked with more popular singers. Some days her dream of becoming a singer felt more like a nightmare.

Leigh's gaze strayed to the photo of her parents sitting on the dresser and she wondered how they were faring. A measure of guilt rose inside her. Outside of the note she'd left, she hadn't written to let them know where she lived or how she was doing and figured they might be worried. She also hoped the school had found a good teacher. She'd left the principal a note, along with six months worth of lesson plans, just in case it took longer than expected. Then there was Percy. She wanted to stay as far away from him as possible. Hopefully by now, he had married some other gullible woman he promised to make famous. She had often thought about writing her parents, but wanted to wait until she'd become successful. Leigh had no desire to hear her father say, "I told you nothing good would come from you singing that devil music." Determined to prove him wrong, she pushed down the melancholy. "I *am* going to be successful." After spending so much time seeing to everyone else's happiness, she was enjoying life on her own terms, even if it meant working hard.

She retrieved the tin box from a drawer and counted the money she had made this week. With tonight's take, Leigh had enough to pay her rent, buy a few groceries, but not much else. She couldn't complain, though, because her rent was reasonable. Most places in Harlem charged members of the race three and four times more than their White counterparts, if they rented to them at all. She'd seen ads specifically barring Negros from applying. Her best friend, Elizabeth Bryant owned the building where Leigh lived, housing a profitable restaurant and catering business downstairs and four apartments upstairs. Liz's parents had migrated to New York from Arkansas during the World War and made a fortune. Upon their deaths, everything had passed down to Liz.

Leigh placed the tin back into the drawer and headed to the bathroom to take a bath. A knock on the door stopped her. The clock on the night table read one-thirty. *Who's knocking on my door this late?* She dearly hoped it wasn't one of the patrons from downstairs. Every now and again, one would somehow get into the building and venture up to the apartments looking for the man who lived two doors down. She walked back to the front door.

"Who is it?"

"It's me, Liz."

Leigh unbolted the door. "Is everything okay?" she asked, searching her friend's face. "Come in."

Liz entered, took a seat in one of the chairs and leaned her head back. "Lord, I'm tired. Why did I decide to open a club?"

She sat on the sofa and laughed. Six months ago, Liz had expanded the restaurant to include a club—aptly called The Magnolia Club to honor their hometown—that rivaled the ones downtown. "Did you come up to catch your breath or is there something else?"

"I'm going to need a full-time singer starting next week. Irene told me tonight that she's moving back to Chicago."

Leigh's eyes widened. "*Really?* When is she leaving?" Irene Fields was a popular jazz and blues singer who had kept The Magnolia packed every night. Liz had graciously allowed Leigh to sing a couple nights a week on the bill.

"Tuesday is her last night. She's leaving at the end of next week."

"Do you have anyone in mind to replace her?"

Liz sat up. "As a matter of fact I do. You."

"*Me?* I don't know, Liz. I mean—"

She lifted a brow. "Are you telling me you *can't* do it or you *won't*?"

"I'm not saying that." Leigh stood and paced. This was the opportunity she had been waiting for. A moment of panic flared. What if she couldn't do it?

"The pay is thirty dollars a week."

Leigh stopped pacing and spun around.

Liz chuckled. "I thought that would get your attention. Leigh, you've been working hard to make a name for yourself and I've seen the response from the audience. They love you. And so do I," she added.

Leigh smiled. Liz was the sister she never had. They had grown up together, went to the same school and sang in the church choir. "I love you, too. And I'll take the job." The promised pay meant Leigh didn't have to worry about making the rent or singing in dangerous places anymore. It also meant she could fatten up her meager wardrobe. She and Liz shared a smile. *Success, here I come.*

* * *

Miles Cooper sat in a shadowy corner of The Magnolia Club Wednesday evening listening to the woman singing on the stage and felt the familiar tug in his chest. Rich, brown skin with eyes to match, full lips painted a deep shade of red, and enough curves beneath the knee-length black flapper to keep a man busy for weeks. She was even more beautiful than he remembered. After roaming for the past three years, he couldn't stay away any longer. It hadn't taken much to find her. He remembered her mentioning staying with her friend, Elizabeth Bryant and everyone in town knew about the restaurant. He found out that she had only added the club a few months ago. On the other nights he'd been there, Leigh shared the stage with another woman and only sang two or three songs. Tonight, however, he had been pleased to hear the announcement that she would be taking over as the house singer.

He closed his eyes and concentrated on her sultry voice. Miles always wondered how this small woman could possess such a powerful voice. He'd been drawn to it from the moment they met and it had haunted him since he'd left her. He hadn't wanted to part that way, but the restlessness that plagued him since childhood had been so overwhelming that he'd had no choice. He had been on the road with his father since the age of four and didn't know another life. Now he was tired of moving from place to place with nowhere to call home. And he missed Leigh. Missed her more than he could have ever imagined.

"You want another drink, honey?"

Miles took a long drag on the cigarette and slowly blew out the smoke. "No, thanks."

The woman, who had identified herself as Belinda the first night he'd come to the club two weeks ago smiled. "And my other offer?"

"Still no." Belinda had expressed her interest in him, but he had eyes for only one woman. Though he didn't expect a warm welcome when he made his presence known.

Her smile faded. She snatched up his empty glass and stormed off.

He refocused his attention on the stage where Leigh was singing a fast-paced jazz tune and frowned. She hit all the right notes and had the audience eating out the palm of her hand, but something about her voice seemed to be missing. It took him a minute to figure it out. Passion. He couldn't *feel* her words. Taking another drag on his cigarette, he contemplated what to do. She had the potential to become one of the greatest singers in the world and he couldn't understand why she had chosen to suppress her talent. As she continued to sing, Miles sat there deciding what course to take. As he'd noted before, Leigh would not be happy to see him. Memories of the way she felt in his arms and the softness of her lips against his surfaced in his mind. He had no idea how he would accomplish it, but he needed to see her, to touch and kiss her again.

Leigh finished the next song and announced a short break. Coming to a decision, Miles stubbed out the cigarette into the ashtray and stood. It was time the crowd got a taste of Leigh's full power. And he knew just the song.

* * *

"Girl, you were fabulous!" Liz smiled. "I knew you could do it."

Leigh stared at Liz through the mirror of the dressing room that Irene used as she sat blotting the moisture from her forehead, a smile playing around her lips. "Did you see the audience?" Folks had clapped, stomped their feet and danced. Watching them had given Leigh more energy and she'd enjoyed every moment of being on the stage.

"I did. And when word gets out about how good you are, I'm gonna have to add more space."

She laughed.

"Pretty soon one of those big recording companies will be offering you a deal."

"That would be something." Leigh leaned back against the chair. A few years ago, record companies realized that Negro music would be popular. When the Okeh Record Company recorded Mamie Smith's Crazy Blues in 1920, the record sold over a million copies in just a year. Now companies like Columbia and Paramount also offered deals to singers and musicians of the race and Leigh wanted to see her name on one of them.

"I'll let you get ready for your next set. Be sure to end it with Tain't Nobody's Business If I Do."

The song made popular by Bessie Smith was one of Leigh's favorites and she sang it most nights. Leigh stood and squeezed Liz's hand. "Thank you so much for giving me this chance. I don't know how I'm ever going to repay you."

"Just keep singing and filling the house. That'll be thanks enough." They shared a smile and Liz departed.

Leigh stared at her reflection. The young woman staring back at her had changed considerably over the past three years. By society standards, she should have been married with children and following the lead of her husband, but she wanted more for herself. She was a college graduate, a teacher and now a jazz and blues singer, just as she had envisioned. Women were doing more than just sitting at home. They had even gotten the vote in 1920. She patted her hair and clipped the silk magnolia flower that had become her signature just above her left ear. Leigh surveyed her look. Her mother would probably have a heart attack if she saw her wearing a dress that left her arms and knees bare. Smoothing it down, she inhaled and went back to the stage.

Thunderous applause greeted her. She glanced around at the small band—Frank Dixon on piano, Samuel White on drums, Willie Young on trumpet and Loyce Douglas on clarinet—and smiled. The men were accomplished musicians and she knew Liz paid them well to perform as the house band. The music started and, once again, Leigh was transported to the place that gave her the most pleasure. She sang a mixture of jazz and blues tunes that kept the audience out of their seats.

The next song started and Leigh froze. She'd recognize that piano style anywhere. *It can't be.* Her heart started pounding. She whipped her head around and her gaze collided with the one man she thought she'd never see again. Leigh's breath stalled in her lungs. Miles smiled. She didn't. She was so stunned she couldn't utter a sound. His smooth voice floated across the space. Finally, she gathered herself and jumped in to sing the second verse of the blues duet they had written together. Before she knew it, they sang with a passion reserved for the two lovers described in the song.

When the song ended, Frank resumed his place at the piano. She finished her set and retreated to the dressing room. She scrubbed a hand across her forehead. Why in the world was Miles here? It had taken her months to forget about him and now he had the nerve to reappear. As far as she was concerned, he could go back to wherever he came from because she had no intention of starting up with him again. Leigh stayed in the room until the club closed thirty minutes later, confident that he would be gone.

Miles sat at the table closest to the stage and his was the first face she saw when she came back inside the club. Her steps slowed. She stopped in front of him. "What are you doing here, Miles?" The musicians stopped packing up their instruments, the servers paused in wiping down the tables and Liz watched her warily from behind the bar.

"I came to see you, baby," he said softly.

He smiled again and something inside of Leigh snapped. She punched him in the jaw, knocking him backwards in the chair. "Go back to wherever you came from." Ignoring the stunned looks on everyone's faces, she spun on her heel and strode out.

Upstairs in her apartment, Leigh paced angrily. Her hand throbbed and would probably be sore for a few days. How dare he waltz back into her life as if he hadn't walked away without any explanation? Things were finally going her way and she did not need this disruption. She hoped he heeded her warning and left. Leigh removed the flower from her hair and placed it on the dresser. She started to change, but heard a knock on the door. Groaning, she went to open it.

"I thought you might need this," Liz said, handing her a towel with ice.

"Thanks." She stepped back for her to enter.

Liz followed her back to the bedroom and sat on the bed. "So, that's Miles. How did he know you were here?"

"I have no idea. He knew I was coming to Harlem, so I guess it wasn't that hard."

"I wonder why he's here."

"I don't care why he's here," Leigh said. "I just want him to leave me alone so I can get on with my life."

"I can understand that. But he is a handsome devil," Liz said with a grin.

Leigh glared.

Liz chuckled. "Don't glare at me. And I don't ever remember you being a brawler."

"One of the guys who kept the peace at Mr. Butler's place was a distant cousin of Jack Johnson and said that a pretty lady should always be able to protect herself, so he taught me a few things." Jack Johnson was the first Negro heavyweight boxing champion and held the title from 1908 until 1915. "This was the first time I've used it."

"Well, I'm sure Miles will think twice about crossing you again. By the way, he's still downstairs. He wants to talk to you."

Leigh sighed. She didn't want to talk to him.

"Do you want him to come up?"

"No," she said quickly. "I know you're closing, but can we talk down there? It won't be long."

Liz stood. "Sure. It'll take another half an hour to clean up, so you have a little time." She pointed at the photo of Leigh's parents. "Have you thought any more about writing to them?"

She had confessed to missing her parents and wondering how they were doing. "I've been thinking on it, but wanted to wait until I made it big."

"Yeah, they'd probably keel over if they saw you on the stage," Liz said with a laugh. "Then they'd haul you right over to the church for the pastor and deacons to pray you back to a holy state."

Leigh snorted. "Girl, please. The only thing holy at that church is the sign on the door. And maybe Mother Harris." The pastor and a few of the deacons had been regular patrons at Mr. Butler's saloon. She'd kept their secret and they'd kept hers. She shook her head. "Anyway, let's get this over with." The sooner she had the conversation, the sooner she'd be rid of him.

She followed Liz back downstairs to where Miles sat with the ice pack against his jaw. She took the chair across from him and waited with her arms folded.

Miles set the ice pack on the table and rubbed his jaw. "You pack a helluva punch, Mae Lee." At her glare, he hastily corrected himself. "Sorry, Leigh." He stared at her a long moment, then said, "You look good, girl."

So did he, but she refused to say so. With his golden skin, towering height and blinding good looks, women constantly threw themselves in his path. "How did you find me?"

"I remembered you saying you were going to stay with your friend, Elizabeth whose parents owned a restaurant. I asked around and it was fairly easy to find her, since the restaurant is well-known. I didn't expect the club."

"She just opened it six months ago. Why did you come here?"

"I missed you, Leigh," Miles said quietly. "Missed you more than you'll ever know."

Despite her anger, her heart skipped a beat. "I need to change." She stood.

He stood and placed a staying hand on her arm. "I'll go with you."

"There's no need. I live upstairs."

"Will you come back and talk to me? I want to try to explain."

As much as she shouldn't care, a part of her wanted to know why he had disappeared. She nodded. Leigh reasoned that if she knew why he left, she could move on with her life. They both could.

CHAPTER 2

Miles placed the ice pack on his sore jaw and waited for Leigh to return. He had expected her to be angry, but he hadn't expected her to land a punch that would do a boxer proud. Elizabeth had introduced herself when she handed him the ice, but outside of that hadn't said another word. Now she stood behind the bar watching him intently.

Belinda came over to the table again and placed a hand on his shoulder. "Is there anything I can do for you?"

"No. I'll be fine." She had been hovering since Leigh stormed out the first time.

"You can come by my place and I'll fix you right up."

"Belinda, are you done cleaning your tables?" Elizabeth asked from the bar.

"Yes."

"Then I'll see you tomorrow. The man said he's fine."

She mumbled something like good night, grabbed up her belongings and walked out.

"Thanks," Miles said.

"You're welcome. What are your intentions with Leigh?"

He studied her. "That's between me and Leigh."

"Not if it interferes with my business."

Elizabeth stood a good eight or nine inches taller than Leigh's five-foot height, had a pretty light brown face and full figure. She also didn't mince words.

"I don't plan to interfere in your business."

"That's good to know." She gave him a meaningful look.

Before he could reply, Leigh entered. Her face still held some anger, but it didn't distract from her beauty. She had changed into a simple white blouse and dark calf-length skirt. She'd also wiped off the lipstick. He remembered how her soft lips felt against his, the sweet taste of her kiss, the melodic sounds of pleasure he'd drawn from her. He would give anything to do it all again.

"Did you sell my music sheets?" Leigh asked as she sat.

Miles shook his head. He had taken three songs when he left, two they had done together and one she had written.

"Then why did you take them?"

He tried to come up with a way to explain that he needed some kind of connection to her after leaving. "I just wanted something to remember you by."

"You had me. That wasn't enough?"

"It was enough, Leigh. More than enough. My leaving had nothing to do with you and I'm so sorry I hurt you. That was never my intention."

"How long do you plan to stay?"

More than anything, he wanted to tell her he'd stay as long as she was there, but he couldn't. Not yet. "I don't know."

"Well, stay out of my way and I'll stay out of yours." Leigh stood and held out her hand. "My music."

Miles reached down for the satchel next to his feet, extracted some papers and handed them to her. He caught her hand. "I would never sell these, baby."

She snatched her hand away. "Don't call me that."

"Leigh—"

Leigh shook her head. "Just stay away from me." She turned to leave.

"Can't do that."

She stopped and faced him. "What are you talking about?"

21

"Exactly what I said. If I could stay away, I wouldn't be here." It didn't matter that she was angry with him or acted like she never wanted to see him again. He couldn't blame her. He'd left her on her own to travel to an unknown place. He hadn't been there her like he should have and he would go to his grave regretting his actions. Anything could have happened to her. She stared at him, seemingly searching for some meaning. But he didn't know what it all meant, either. He only knew he wanted to be near her. "It's late. We can talk some other time."

"We'll see."

Miles smiled. "Yeah, we will. Good night, Leigh." He watched until she disappeared through the back door.

Liz came over and placed a glass in front of him. "You look like you could use this."

He tossed the drink back, set the glass on the table with a thud and stood. "No. I need more than this." While putting on his hat, he contemplated asking her how much for the bottle, thinking if he got drunk enough, it would dampen his desire for Leigh. Unlike the foul taste of bathtub gin, which was known to kill a person, Liz's liquor reminded him of the whiskey before prohibition. Undoubtedly, she knew a good bootlegger. In the end, he decided against it. Spirits dulled the mind and he liked to stay sharp. He tipped his hat politely to Liz and walked out the front door and down the three blocks to his apartment.

The place Miles called his temporary home didn't have much in the way of furniture and it suited him just fine. As long as he had a bed and a place to cook, he would make do. Moving around as often as he did taught him to be frugal and whenever it became time to leave again, everything he owned could fit into one suitcase. He removed his father's pocket watch and a photo of his parents on their wedding day from his pants and placed them on the night table next to the bed. Miles fingered his father's wedding band resting on the fourth finger of his left hand. His father told him that his mother had insisted on purchasing him one and didn't care whether it was popular or not. They were the only things he had left of his parents. His mother died when he was three and he had no memory of her. Afterward he and his father lived with Miles's paternal grandmother in Louisiana for about six months. But his father was so brokenhearted over losing his wife he turned to the one thing that made him happy—music. Miles Cooper, Sr. packed up and hit the road, taking Miles with him. Miles remembered never staying in one place for more than three or four months, but, somehow, they always had a roof over their heads and food to eat. He recalled sitting on his father's lap learning to play the piano.

When Miles was old enough, he played alongside his father in the various saloons and clubs. The attention he garnered often resulted in a few extra dollars, which his father promptly tucked away, telling Miles that money was for Miles's future. But those times had passed. His father went off to fight in the World War and came home in a pine box. Miles had been eighteen at the time and went back to Louisiana to stay with his grandmother. He found a job working on a farm, but he couldn't live without the music and soon found himself wandering again. Restless feet, his grandmother had called it. She also told him it would take a good woman to settle him, just like it had done his father. However, he didn't put any stock in her words because he'd met several women and none held his interest for long. Until Leigh. After leaving, he'd had a few dalliances, but always found them lacking. Not so with Leigh. From her sparkling dark eyes and playful smile to her sassy ways and smooth voice, she had touched a chord in his heart. But he'd hurt her and he had to take his comeuppance like a man. He didn't know anything about putting down roots, but in order to have her he would have to learn.

* * *

Leigh woke up the next morning in a foul mood. She'd tossed and turned all night thinking about Miles. Pushing him out of her mind, she took care of her needs, dressed and went out to run her errands. One of the things she enjoyed most about Harlem was everything being in walking distance. She stopped to speak to the West Indian couple who owned the market and headed over to the produce section to see if they had any peaches. She was just about out of her beloved peach jam and wanted to make more. They had a nice selection, so she got a few more to put up for the winter. Leigh added some more things to her basket, paid for her purchases and reversed her course for home. On the way back, she admired an evening dress in the window of a shop. Now that she had a bit more money coming in, she would treat herself to something nice soon.

Once she returned to her apartment, Leigh started the arduous task of doing laundry. It had never been one of her favorite chores. She didn't have many clothes, but after adding the bedding and towels, she felt like she had washed clothes for an entire family. She hung everything on the clothesline downstairs behind the building, except her underthings. Those she hung in the bathroom. Leigh changed out of her wet blouse then went downstairs to have lunch with Liz in the restaurant.

"I was wondering where you were," Liz said.

"Laundry. I think my clothes multiply when I'm not looking," Leigh added with a chuckle.

"I still have to do mine. Thank goodness we're closed tonight." The club was closed on Thursdays and Sundays, while the restaurant only closed on Sundays. A server came to take their order. They spent a few minutes discussing some new ideas Liz had for the club.

"So you and Miles talked for a while last night. Did he say why he's here?"

Leigh fiddled with the napkin in her lap. "He said he missed me, but I wasn't born yesterday."

"You don't believe him?"

Her brow lifted. "Would you? He's been gone three years, Liz." She paused when the server came and placed the food on the table. She thanked the woman and picked up her fork. "If you miss somebody, it doesn't take that long to figure out."

Liz shrugged. "Maybe he couldn't afford to come until now."

"Why are you taking his side?"

"I'm not. I'm just saying he may have a good reason."

"If he does, he didn't share it with me." Leigh couldn't come up with one plausible scenario as to why Miles had disappeared for three years and hadn't made an attempt to find her until now.

"Whatever the case," she said between bites, "the man can play that piano and sing."

Yes, he could. She'd heard his voice in her dreams all night long. Deciding they needed to change the subject, she asked, "Are you going to Mrs. Perkins's rent party tonight?" A man had handed her a rent party ticket while out that morning.

"Probably. Her husband lost his job a couple of weeks ago, so I know they need the money."

"I didn't know that. I hope he finds something soon." Neighbors brought all kinds of foods, supplied bootleg liquor, and had piano players or a small band. People paid an admission fee and extra for food and drinks. One could find a party every night, but most took place on a Saturday when laborers got paid and didn't have to work the next day. Those had been Leigh's best money-making nights. Thursdays had gained popularity lately because most sleep-in domestic workers had the day off. "I'll go with you."

Later, Leigh met Liz and Frank downstairs for the ride over. She could hear the loud voices and smell the food as soon as they entered the building. They handed their twenty-five cents to the woman at the door and squeezed into the crowded space. The regular lights had been replaced with soft, colored ones. All the furniture had been moved from the front room and the rugs taken up, leaving only a piano. Frank immediately slid onto the bench and started playing. Leigh and Liz found their way to the kitchen where the hosts were serving fried chicken, pork chops, potato salad, chitterlings, Hoppin' John, collard greens and gumbo. Liz paid the additional ten cents for a plate, but Leigh declined.

She ventured back to the front room to watch the dancing. She tapped her foot and clapped in time with the rhythm until a young man she knew from the restaurant pulled her out onto the floor. They did the Charleston, Jitterbug and Lindyhop, and had a great time. Her partner spun her out. Her laughter faded and she missed a step. Miles stood leaning against the wall watching her, his expression unreadable. Leigh quickly gathered herself and continued dancing, angry that his mere presence could rattle her. Without turning around, she could feel his heated gaze and, after another minute, she excused herself from her dance partner and wound her way through the apartment to the bathroom.

A man latched on to her arm. "Hey, honey. One of the bedrooms is free. How 'bout you and me—"

Leigh jerked her arm away and stared, appalled. "I beg your pardon, sir! I am *not* that kind of girl." Along with the food and dancing, at many parties, the bedrooms were reserved for gambling and other illicit activities.

The man ducked his head and had the decency to look embarrassed. He mumbled something that sounded like, "My apologies, ma'am," and shuffled off down the hallway.

"Honey, you know you can earn three days' pay or more in just fifteen minutes. It ain't bad."

She stared in utter shock at the scantily dressed woman lounging against the opposite wall.

"Hmph. I'd be a fool to go back to cleaning and scrubbing and breaking my back all day." She shrugged. "Just something to think about." She sauntered off.

Leigh shook her head. She would never resort to working on her back to for any reason. She closed the bathroom door, leaned against it and took a deep breath. Her mind went back to Miles. This wasn't exactly what she had in mind when she told Miles to stay out of her way. She didn't want to keep bumping into him all over the city. Seeing him reminded her too much of their times together—the music, the dancing, the kisses. She promptly dismissed the latter thought. There would be no kissing this time around. Leigh wished she could stay in the bathroom all night, or at least until he left. Sighing, she went back to join the party.

Before she could take two steps, a hand slid around her waist and Leigh turned, intending to give the offender a blistering retort.

"Holster your weapons, baby. I only want to dance," Miles whispered close to her ear.

Dancing with him could prove to be very dangerous, especially since the music had changed from the energy-filled jazz to the sultry blues. Couples all over the room snuggled

27

close and swayed slowly to the music, and some men had their women against the wall, stealing kisses. No, dancing would *not* be a good idea. He extended his hand and she reluctantly let herself be led onto the floor. The moment Miles pulled her into his arms, all rational thought left her head. Leigh tried to remain distant, but the heat of his body against hers seeped through to her skin, warming her all over. The sound of his steady heartbeat beneath her ear melted her resistance and she lost herself in his embrace. His hand made an unhurried path up her spine and her pulse skipped. No other man had touched her this way and as much as she tried to deny it, she'd missed him.

"I missed holding you this way," he said, echoing her thoughts. "I know I hurt you, but give me another chance to show you I'm a changed man."

Leigh lifted her head and met his gaze. Lord knew it would be easy to fall back into a relationship with him, but one heartbreak was enough to last her a lifetime. "I don't think that's a good idea, Miles. I—"

"We were good together and I know we'll be even better this time." He gathered her closer and continued to dance until the last notes of the song faded away. "Thanks for the dance, Leigh."

"You're welcome." Without taking his eyes off her, he lifted her hand and brought it to his lips in a soft, lingering kiss that sent heat flowing up her arm. He smiled, inclined his head and left her standing in the middle of the floor trying to breathe again. She glanced around and saw a few raised eyebrows, as well as two women glaring at her, one being Belinda from the restaurant. Liz had mentioned the woman staying around to try to talk to Miles last night.

"Hey, Miss Leigh," someone called from the crowd. "Come on up and sing something."

Leigh hadn't come to sing. In fact, she planned to make a hasty exit. But the group didn't give her a choice. She pasted a smile on her face and moved to the piano to talk to Frank. However, Miles was the one at the piano. He didn't even ask which song, just started playing the same blues song he had at the club. The response from the audience mirrored that of the one last night and they ended up singing two more songs. Sure she'd been compensated, but that wasn't the point.

She moved through the crowd and found Liz. "I'm ready to leave. Where's Frank?"

Liz gave her an exasperated look. "He's in the back room."

"Gambling or…?"

"Gambling, but I don't know why because he loses every time. We can catch a ride with someone else. Unless you want to ask Miles. I'm sure he wouldn't mind."

She held up a hand. "Don't start."

"What?" Liz asked with mock innocence, her amusement plain.

"Not one word, Liz. Not one." Leigh fumed all the way home. What he'd done would be all over Harlem by morning. Granted, she could have pulled her hand away and avoided the entire scene, but Miles had a way of leaving her at such sixes and sevens she couldn't remember her own name half of the time. She sighed. With any luck, folks would chalk it all up to them having a good time. But that still didn't solve   her   problem.

CHAPTER 3

Miles viewed Leigh's departure knowingly. He'd felt the way her hands held him around the neck, heard her breathless sighs. Their attraction might be mutual, but she was right. He needed to back away if he couldn't promise her he would stay. And right now he couldn't. He turned his attention back to the piano, the one place that gave him peace and played for another hour. Afterward, he collected his fee and purchased a plate of food. While eating, he stood off to the side conversing with another musician he'd met. He hadn't had fried pork chops this good since leaving his grandmother's house and almost went back to purchase a couple more.

A woman sidled up next to them "You boys look like you could use a little company." She rattled off the price for fifteen minutes in the bedroom.

Miles declined, but the other man followed her back with a smile. Shaking his head, he finished his food and got a glass of lemonade. A loud commotion from the back interrupted the party. Women screamed and a surge of people streamed by, trying to get out of the path of the combatants. Miles saw the two home defense officers who had been hired to keep the peace rush in the direction of the yelling and he went the opposite way. He had no desire to get caught up in whatever dispute was taking place. The last time a brawl had broken out at one of these gatherings, he gotten trapped in the middle and ended up with a slash across his forearm that kept him from playing the piano for weeks.

He set the glass down on a nearby table, slipped out the door, unnoticed, and hustled down the steps to the front of the building. While walking to his Model T Ford, the only substantial purchase he had made, he lit a cigarette. Having a car allowed him to escape some of the Jim Crow laws inflicted on members of the race when traveling by train. Miles had been put off simply because of his race more times than he could count. He still ran into problems while driving on the road, from being denied a room and a meal, and being allowed to buy gas but not use the bathroom to being stopped by the police for no apparent reason. He learned to carry food, blankets and an empty coffee can at all times. And to avoid certain areas, especially at night.

Miles drove to his place, picked up the two pieces of mail from his box and went upstairs. One envelope bore his grandmother's distinctive flowing handwriting. He had promised to always let her know where he'd be and he had written to her upon his arrival three weeks ago. He smiled. The second envelope had his name on it, but no address. Curious, he opened it first. As he read, his grin widened. A local band needed a piano player for a few nights and the leader wanted to meet with Miles tomorrow to discuss it. But if he got the job, it would mean not seeing Leigh. She'd get her wish, at least for a short time. Miles noted the time and place, set the note aside and opened the letter from his grandmother. She let him know that she had received his letter and reminded him that she was getting up in age and he should make plans to visit soon.

Miles wondered what his grandmother would think of Leigh. Both were cut from the same cloth and possessed a determination he didn't often see. His grandmother had raised six sons alone after his grandfather died in a tractor accident, and Leigh had moved away from everything she had known to pursue her dreams. He hadn't seen Mama, as he called her, in over six months and probably needed to make that trip. But he worried what Leigh would think if he

31

left again. She most likely wouldn't believe that he'd come back. Miles briefly toyed with asking her to accompany him, but decided it wouldn't sit well with her, especially without a commitment. He had no business even thinking about inviting her. He ran a hand over his face. He had really made a mess of things and didn't know how to fix them, or if he even could. He would think on it more later. For now, he climbed into bed and turned off the lamp. He had a job to see about tomorrow.

* * *

Friday morning, Miles dressed and went to meet the man who had left the note. He entered the restaurant and questioned a hostess, who pointed out Oscar Porter seated across the room. Miles thanked her and made his way over to the table. "Mr. Porter?"

The man looked up from his newspaper and coffee. "Yes."

He extended his hand. "Miles Cooper."

A wide grin covered his face. "Yes, yes. Please have a seat, and call me Oscar." He folded up the paper and placed it next to his plate. "Have you eaten yet?"

"Yes, sir." The dark-skinned Oscar looked to be a decade older than Miles's twenty-eight years, had a raspy voice and wore his hair slicked back.

"Well, let's get right to it. My piano player has been laid low for a few days with a fever and the band is scheduled to play at the Cotton Club starting tonight for a week. A friend of mine heard you playing over at the Magnolia Club and suggested I get in touch. Are you a regular there?"

The Cotton Club? Miles kept his excitement hidden. "No, sir. I'm in between jobs right now." He listened as Oscar laid out the details and felt his eyes widen at the salary. He'd make more money in a week than he ever had. The Cotton Club had been previously owned by ex-boxer Jack Johnson and called Club De Luxe.

Owney Madden, a known gangster had taken it over in 1923 and given it its current name. He had a Whites only policy, except for the entertainment and staff. The dancers for his floorshow had to be light-skinned, at least five feet, six inches tall and under twenty-one years old.

"How are you at improvising?"

"The best you'll ever find." Miles's father taught him well and Miles was ahead of his time when it came to music. They both smiled. Oscar told him more about his band. The ten-piece Oscar Porter Orchestra had been together for five years and was considered one of many territory bands that traveled around playing one-nighters. Miles wanted to ask how they happened upon the Cotton Club gig, but held his question. From all the information Oscar related, it appeared that the band had become pretty popular. He did ask about where to meet and at what time, as well as whether they had uniforms.

"No uniforms. Just a black suit, white shirt and black bow tie. The one you're wearing will work just fine. Anything else?"

"No, sir."

"Then I'll see you tonight." Oscar rose to his feet.

Miles followed suit and noted that Oscar stood a good four inches shorter than his own six-foot height. The two men shook hands and Miles left Oscar to finish his coffee. He wasn't particularly fond of bow ties, preferring the silk necktie. However, for fifty-five dollars, he'd pretend. He stopped a men's clothing shop on the way home to purchase one and spent time making sure his suit was pressed just so and his shoes buffed to a shine. Miles thought about stopping in to see Leigh before heading over, but changed his mind. He only had an hour and it wouldn't be nearly enough time. Besides, she had to sing tonight, as well. Too bad he couldn't bring her along with him. They made magic together and he had to find a way to prove it to her.

He arrived at the building on the corner of Lennox Avenue and 142nd Street at the appointed time and Oscar introduced him to the other band members. Most were welcoming, but two seemed skeptical, which was understandable since none had ever heard him play.

Miles had his first look inside the Cotton Club minutes later. There were two levels of tables placed in the shape of a horseshoe, murals painted on the walls, fake palm trees filled corners and Colored waiters in red tuxedos moved amongst the sea of White faces dressed in their finery and jewels. He scanned the stage area and his eyes widened slightly. The bandstand had been set a few steps up from the main floor and had large white columns. Weeping willows and slave quarters were painted on the wall. It felt as if he had stumbled onto a mansion on a southern slave plantation. His gut churned at the sight and he turned away.

By the end of the second night, Miles's initial enthusiasm had waned considerably. The mood and style of music had him feeling like some exotic animal on display in a jungle. He would finish his commitment to the band, but doubted he would perform there again. Because the club opened at nine for dinner and dancing, the floor shows starting around midnight and the final performance ending right before the three in the morning closing, he hadn't had a chance to see Leigh and he missed her terribly. But he planned to rectify that Friday night, as soon as he was done.

* * *

"What do you mean Frank can't play the piano?" Leigh leaned forward on the barstool. She had come down to keep Liz company Friday evening before the dinner crowd arrived.

Liz exhaled deeply and placed another glass on the shelf. "Gambling. The fool got into a scuffle over something after we left the Perkins's apartment last Thursday."

Her brows knit in confusion. "That was a week ago. He's been playing fine since then." Friday night was one of the busiest evenings and if they didn't have a piano player, Liz might have to cancel the show.

"Apparently, he owed some money and the men came to collect last night. He didn't have it. They beat him pretty badly." She shook her head and released a deep sigh. "I told him over and over to stop playing with those men."

"So did I," Leigh said sadly. Some of them were tied to the gangsters around the city. She felt bad for Frank and wished he had listened to them. "Is he going to be okay?"

"I hope so. But that means I need to find another piano player." Liz paused. "Have you seen Miles since last week?"

"No." She assumed he had bowed to her wishes to keep his distance. "Why?" When Liz didn't answer immediately, a sense of dread crept up her spine. "Liz, please don't tell me you're thinking of asking him to take Frank's place."

"Okay, I won't. But do you know anyone better? I don't need to remind you how the audience responded to the two of you. It makes perfect business sense."

Leigh sighed. Her nice life was on the verge of spinning out of control. No way would she be able to resist Miles if she had to see him every night. Although the news didn't make her happy, it would be unfair to interfere in her friend's business. Liz had worked hard to establish her upscale dinner club and had given Leigh the chance to pursue her own dreams in the process. If people stopped coming, Liz would be out of business. And Leigh would be out of a steady job. For the first time since moving, she felt a sense of peace and security and had no desire to mess it up. "What if he left town already?" It wouldn't be the first time he skipped out.

Liz put her hands on her hips and snorted. "Honey, that man ain't going nowhere right now. I'm not blind. The way he looked at you on that dance floor had every woman in the room wishing she were in your shoes. I could feel the heat clear across the room." She fanned herself.

The intensity of his gaze came back to her with vivid clarity. Leigh hadn't been able to get the kiss out of her mind. Her hand tingled in remembrance and she rubbed the spot, willing it to stop. She buried her head in her hands. "Why did he have to show up now, just when I'm finally getting settled?"

"Clearly the man is taken with you and maybe this time things will work out. But, if you want the answer to that question, I suggest you ask him yourself." Liz gestured toward the front door.

She spun on her stool and saw Miles entering. Their eyes met and the corner of his mouth kicked up in a smile. The suit he wore looked to be new, as did the hat, and he still was the most handsome man she'd ever known. Her pulse skipped. *Why does he always affect me this way?* The closer he came, the faster her heart pounded in her chest. She heard Liz's soft laughter. Finally, she tore her gaze away and shifted to face Liz. "What?"

"You. I thought you weren't attracted to him. The way you're staring at him leads me to believe you haven't been honest with me...or yourself."

Leigh opened her mouth to refute the claim, but closed it. She had never had a problem dismissing another man's attentions, but this time, despite her best efforts, nothing worked. She didn't want to be attracted to Miles, but it seemed fate had other plans.

When Miles reached the bar, he removed his hat and nodded a greeting to Liz. Then he slid onto the seat next to Leigh and trained his dark gaze on her. "How've you been, Leigh?"

"Okay. And you?"

"Good."

She wanted to ask where he had been over the past week, but she wasn't supposed to care. Besides, she'd told him to stay away.

"I missed you, girl," Miles said quietly. "And before that mind of yours starts thinking the worst, I had a job over at the Cotton Club, filling in as pianist for the Oscar Porter Orchestra."

Leigh averted her eyes. He'd summed up her thoughts. "That's quite an honor. Are you going to be playing there for a while?" If he had the job there, he couldn't fill in for Frank.

He shook his head. "It was just temporary, until their pianist recovered from an illness. The band will be moving on to another city tomorrow. They asked me to travel with them, but I told them I couldn't go."

"Why?"

"I have a more pressing engagement here. You."

She hazarded a glance Liz's way and Liz gave her a look that said, "I told you so."

Miles grasped her hand. "I know you asked me to stay away, and I tried, God knows I did, but it's not working, sweetheart."

Leigh really needed him to stop looking at her like this. His sincere expression was making it hard to fight her feelings for him.

"So, Miles," Liz said, coming back their way, "did I hear you say you don't have a job right now?"

"Yes, ma'am."

"I'm in need of a piano player who can start immediately."

He divided a glance between Leigh and Liz. "What happened to Frank?"

Liz told him the same thing she'd told Leigh.

"Damn," he whispered. "I didn't know he was involved in the scuffle."

"You were there?" Leigh asked.

"At the start, but I hightailed it out of there before it spilled into the front room."

"What does that mean?"

"Let's just say I didn't want to get caught in the middle of something that wasn't my concern and come out on the short end again."

Had he been injured in a brawl? Leigh searched his face. "You were hurt?"

"I'm good. So, what about this job, Miss Liz?"

"I just need to know if you want it. I can't afford to lose business with all these new places cropping up."

"How long will you need me?"

"At least a month. I doubt Frank will be up and around before then. And did I tell you the pay?" She wrote down something on a piece of paper and slid it across the bar.

She knew Liz would offer him a salary that guaranteed a yes answer.

Miles smiled and glanced at Leigh before saying, "Miss Liz, you've got yourself a piano player for as long as you need."

Liz smiled and clapped her hands. "Thank you."

Leigh didn't know whether to shout *Hallelujah!* or get as far away from him as possible.

"You think we can go for a walk, Leigh?" Miles asked. "We won't go far."

She hesitated briefly. "Sure." He offered his hand to help her down, but didn't let go. He escorted her out the front of the restaurant and they started a leisurely stroll up the street. For the first few minutes neither spoke. People they passed spoke or nodded and she responded in kind.

"Are you okay with me taking this job?"

Her steps slowed and she glanced up at him. "If I wasn't would you reconsider?"

He didn't answer.

Leigh eased her hand from his and picked up the pace again. "I'm sorry. That's not fair. I know how much music means to you and I'll do anything to help Liz. She took me in when I got here, made sure I had a place to stay and helped me get on my feet. Now she's offered me a chance to headline at her club when she could have found someone far more popular. So, yes, I'm fine with anything that will keep the doors open."

"She seems like a nice lady."

"She's been like a sister to me." She thought it a good time to bring up their relationship. "I think we should stick with just working together and concentrate on giving the audience a good show."

Miles glanced down at her. "Do you now? What if I told you I don't think that's going to happen?"

"Why wouldn't it?" She waved at a woman she had met a few months ago at a poetry reading.

"Because you're as affected by me as I am you."

Leigh faced him and put a hand on her hip. "I am not." Miles took two steps away. "What are you doing?"

"Moving out of the way so I don't get struck by lightning from the lie you just told," he said with a chuckle.

She couldn't stop the laughter that spilled from her lips. "Oh, hush."

Miles took her hand again and pulled her into a sweet shop. "Can I tempt you with a bowl of vanilla ice cream? I know it's your favorite."

She stared at him in wonder. "You remembered?"

"Sweetheart, I remember everything about you. So?"

It took her a moment to process his words. "What did you just say?"

"I asked if you wanted ice cream."

"Not that."

He repeated it. "I know that you like ice cream, dunk your toast in your coffee and can make a prize-winning apple pie." He moved closer and reached for a strand of her hair. "I know that you love reading and art sculptures and that you twirl your hair around your finger when you're thinking or when something is bothering you," he continued passionately. "More?"

Leigh couldn't form an answer to save her life. Had he really paid that much attention to her in the few months that they had been together?

"I remember your sounds of pleasure when I touch you and kiss you."

Her knees turned to jelly. "I...I think we should get that ice cream." She snatched open the door and left him standing there. She drew in a deep breath and tried to calm her runaway heartbeat. Keeping him at a distance would be harder than she ever imagined.

CHAPTER 4

Wednesday evening, Miles dressed for the show at the Magnolia Club and smiled. For four nights, he and Leigh had given performances that kept the audience coming back. More and more people squeezed into the space to hear what had been described as the best jazz anywhere uptown. Leigh. Spending time with her had been his only goal when he drove from Chicago to New York and he couldn't have planned it any better. However, they hadn't spent much time together outside of singing since the last Friday when he bought her ice cream.

Miles hadn't meant to say all those things to her yet. He'd wanted her to get used to him being around for a while. But once he started, he couldn't stop. He also wanted her to know he remembered how it felt to have her touch him, how it felt to make love to her. She'd given him her most precious gift—something that should be for a husband—and he should have done more to protect and care for her. Instead, he gave in to the turmoil inside that wouldn't allow him to stay. There had been a couple of other women, but he always ended up comparing them to Leigh. They seemed to sense someone else occupied the space in his heart and didn't mind him moving on. Miles buttoned his vest, laced up his shoes and grabbed his jacket. He didn't want any other woman but her. However, to have her, he would have to change his life and he still didn't know if he could. He grabbed his hat. Maybe it would be best to keep his distance until he figured it out. Then again, he didn't think he could do that, either.

When Miles arrived at the club, he immediately sought out Leigh. A hostess told him he'd find her in the dressing room, so he went and knocked on the door. A moment later, it opened. His gaze traveled from the slight rise of her breasts above the low-cut ivory dress that clung enticingly to her hips and ended a couple of inches above her knees. She had on a matching pair of ivory heels.

"Miles. Hi. Is something wrong?"

"You look beautiful." She gave him a shy smile. "And there's nothing wrong. I just wanted to see you."

Leigh rolled her eyes. "You'll see me in twenty minutes on the stage."

He grinned. "True. But I can't do this on the stage." He bent and brushed his lips across hers. "See you in a bit." Miles hustled himself down the hallway and into the dining area and drew in a couple of deep breaths. Had he stayed one more moment, neither of them would have been on the stage at show time. He wanted to reacquaint himself with the sweet taste of her kiss, the feel of her soft skin and hear her breathless sighs of pleasure. He signaled the bartender. The man came over and poured him a small shot of whiskey, which he promptly downed.

Miles made his way to the stage and took his place to warm up with the band. Fifteen minutes later, the announcer appeared.

"Ladies and gentlemen, let's give a big round of applause for the Magnolia Club band and Miss Leigh Jones."

That was his cue. He launched into the first tune and Leigh strutted out. It was a good thing he knew the songs as well as he knew himself because he couldn't take his eyes off her. At one point, she came and sat next to him on the piano bench as they sang a blues duet. She leaned into him and it took every ounce of his control to keep playing and not haul her into his arms and kiss her like he'd been wanting to since the first day he saw her almost a month ago.

Miles had never been so glad to see the set end. The softness of her curves pressed against him and the sweet smell of her perfume wreaked havoc on his senses. He watched Leigh laugh and mingle and wanted to tell Liz to cancel the next set and send everyone home so he could have her to himself.

"Man, if you don't stop looking at her like that, you're going to burn the place down."

He turned at the sound of the trumpet player's voice. "I don't know what you mean, Willie."

"Leigh. Anybody can see that she's caught your eye." Willie glanced her way, then turned back to Miles. "I can't blame you, though. She's something special."

"Yes, she is," he said, not taking his eyes off her.

Willie laughed and clapped him on the shoulder. "I'm going to get something to drink. You want me to bring you something back?"

"No. I'm good." Finally, Leigh started in his direction. She stopped to talk to Liz before going toward the back door that led to her dressing room. Miles followed her. "You're putting on quite a show tonight."

"That's what they pay me for, isn't it?" Leigh asked with a sassy smile.

"Are you sure it's not something else?"

"Something like what? It's my job to give them what they want," she added with a laugh.

He closed the distance between them. "What about what I want? Will you do the same for me?"

She lowered her head. "I...I thought we agreed to focus on the music and that's all."

"I never agreed to that. I told you before I'm here for you." Miles tilted her chin and stroked a finger down her cheek. "And what I want is this." He lowered his head and kissed her slowly, thoroughly, like he'd dreamed about. He found her kiss just as sweet as he remembered. He slid an arm around her waist, drew her closer and deepened the kiss, her soft curves pressing against his hard body. Feeling himself on the brink of losing control, he eased back, but continued to gift her with fleeting kisses along her jaw and in the hollow of her neck. "You, Leigh. What I want is you." He kissed her once more, then left while he still could.

* * *

Leigh slumped against the wall, her eyes closed and her breathing ragged. The kiss had literally stolen her breath and brought back every moment of their time together. It also reminded her how easily it had been to fall for him. "I can*not* fall for this man again," she muttered, still trying to get control of her runaway pulse. She heard a noise behind her and jumped slightly. Her eyes snapped open. Liz came down the stairs, concern etched in her face.

"You okay, Leigh?"

"Fine," she lied.

Liz studied her, and then smiled.

"What?" Had her hair become mussed when Miles kissed her? Leigh instinctively brought her hand up to smooth down her hair.

"So you and Miles are back together." It was more statement than question.

"No. Miles and I aren't anything." Not exactly the truth, but if she said it enough, maybe she could convince herself.

"You sure about that?" Liz continued her descent and stopped in front of Leigh. "Your lips say something entirely different."

She blinked.

Liz walked past Leigh and called over her shoulder, "Oh, and you might want to fix your lipstick before the next set." She left, her laughter trailing.

Leigh's hand came up to her lips and she immediately snatched it down. "That Miles." She took refuge in her dressing room for the next few minutes. Staring at her lips in the mirror, she noticed they were slightly puffy, her lipstick barely visible. She reapplied the deep ruby color and leaned back in the chair. *You, Leigh. What I want is you.* Miles's words came back to her in a rush. Admittedly, parts of her were flattered that he'd come just to find her. Then again, he could have been lying to get what he wanted. *He's never lied to you before*, an inner voiced chimed. Leigh stood and adjusted her dress. "No, he didn't lie, but he broke my heart." She would do well to remember that.

On stage again, it didn't take much for her to become lost in the music. Music always made her happy in ways nothing else did. Whenever she felt anger or sadness, she would start singing and her mood lifted. Though, she didn't know what kind of mood Miles was trying to rouse in her right now. Earlier, he had accused her of being playful during what had become their signature song. This time he turned the tables on her and she found herself being pulled into a sensual web from which she couldn't escape. His eyes touched her as surely as if it were his hands, and his voice seduced her, beckoning her to let go. Leigh shook herself free of his spell and launched into the final song of the night, an up-tempo feel-good jazz number.

When it was over, she smiled out at the crowd, curtsied then gestured toward the band. Each man bowed. Loyce helped her down from the stage and she went to the bar to get a glass of water. She took a seat at a recently vacated table and, as she sipped, she discreetly took peeks at

Miles as several women surrounded him, smiling flirtatiously. For some reason, the sight bothered her more than she cared to admit. Leigh was fighting a losing battle and she didn't know what to do about it. Fortunately, she had tomorrow off and didn't have to see him. Hopefully, by Friday with some much-needed space, she'd be back on an even keel and better equipped to handle the man.

"Miss Leigh?"

Leigh glimpsed over her shoulder and sighed inwardly. Caleb Smith had been asking her out since the first night she'd sang in the club and she'd politely declined each time. He seemed nice, but he couldn't be a day over eighteen. She wasn't looking to start up with anyone, least of all someone so young. "Hello, Caleb."

Caleb thrust a bunch of wildflowers at her. "These are for you."

She accepted the flowers. "Thank you. They're very nice."

"Thanks," he said with a shy smile. An awkward silence ensued. Finally, he said, "My mom grows the flowers in her garden."

Just as she suspected. She wondered if his mother knew he frequented the dinner club. It was nearly midnight. Again he stood there. "Was there something you wanted, Caleb?" she asked gently.

"I was going to ask you out to dinner again, but you'll probably say no again, so…" He glanced up at her with a hopeful expression.

She shook her head. "Caleb, you're a very nice young man, but I don't think we'd suit." Out of her periphery, she saw Miles headed their way and prayed he would behave.

47

Miles came and stood behind her chair with his hands braced on the top. "Excuse me, Leigh. Do you mind if we discuss Friday's show? I'm about to head out."

Leigh made the introductions. "Miles Cooper this is Caleb Smith. Caleb, Miles."

The men nodded politely.

"I'm sorry, Caleb, but Miles and I need to talk."

"Sure, sure," he said, but his expression said he wasn't too pleased by the interruption. "I'll see you later, Leigh." He stood there another moment, as if he had something else to say, then nodded.

"Good night, Caleb."

He made a hasty retreat and Miles pulled out a chair and sat.

"What did you want to talk about?"

"Another one of your admirers?"

Leigh smiled. "He's a nice young man. He brought me flowers."

Miles's gaze shifted briefly to the flowers then back up at Leigh. "*Young,* being the key word. His mama would keel over if he brought you home, with you singing that devil music and all."

She burst out laughing and swatted Miles on the arm. "That's not a nice thing to say."

"But it's the truth," he said, joining her laughter. He quieted. "So should I bring you flowers?"

"I thought you wanted to talk about the music."

"I lied."

Her mouth fell open. "Miles Cooper, what am I going to do with you?"

He shrugged. "That kid had been talking to you long enough. It seems like you have quite a few men who are sweet on you, if tonight is any indication."

Leigh stared at him. "If I didn't know better, I'd think you were jealous."

"And if I am?"

She had no ready answer. She hadn't encouraged any of her suitors, but that didn't stop them from asking. Was he really jealous?

"I may be crazy and selfish, but I want to be the only man to put a smile on your face, the only one to bring you flowers and ice cream, and anything else your heart desires."

His words touched her. "Oh, Miles."

Miles brought her hand to his lips. "I know I messed up, Leigh, but I want another chance."

Leigh had to look away or drown. His earnest plea had her ready to throw caution to the wind. "I don't want to go through the same thing with you walking away without a backwards glance, leaving only a note."

He released her hand and scrubbed a hand down his face. "I apologized for that, Leigh and I don't envision doing the same thing again."

"You say that now, but what about three months from now?"

"I'm not planning to leave. Unless you're leaving with me." He held out his hand. "Let me prove it to you."

She hesitated before placing her hand in his and hoped she wasn't making a mistake.

"Thank you. May I see you to your door? I don't plan to come in," Miles added. He leaned forward. "But I do want a good night kiss. I figure better there than down here."

The club had virtually emptied, as it would be closing soon. Only a few stragglers remained. If they saw Miles follow her out, gossip would attach itself to her like fleas on a dog.

"I won't be up there long enough for anyone to think anything is going on other than me walking you to your door," he said, as if reading her mind. "I'll even go out the front and come around through the back entrance, if it makes you feel better."

Leigh breathed a sigh of relief. "Thank you." Miles stood and helped her to her feet. She discreetly handed him a key. "This is to the back door." To anyone watching, it would appear as if he were saying goodbye. Only she knew better. She gave him a wave, said good night to those still milling about and exited.

Miles appeared at her door a few minutes later and knocked softly.

She opened the door and saw him leaning against the frame with his hands in his pockets. Without a word, he leaned down and placed a gentle kiss on her lips.

"Good night." He touched his mouth to hers once more, turned and loped down the hallway toward the back stairs.

Leigh closed the door and, with a smile, floated off to bed.

* * *

Leigh completed her laundry and sat down at the table to finally write the letter to her parents. She had no idea how to start, and ended up beginning with an apology for worrying them. She let them know where she lived and that she was well. She ended it by saying she hoped they could forgive her one day. Tears stung her eyes. She missed her parents. Rising, she placed it in the envelope she'd left in her room, picked up her handbag and walked to the post office. Even if they didn't respond, she felt better for having sent it.

Upon her return, she found Miles waiting by her door. She had forgotten she'd given him her spare key. "What are you doing here?" she whispered, taking furtive glances up and down the hall. An older woman who considered herself the moral authority in the building rented the apartment next to Leigh. She turned her nose up at Leigh and Liz, and complained about the music being played in the club. Why she continued to rent in a place owned by "heathens" was beyond Leigh.

"I wanted to see you."

She quickly unlocked her door and ushered him in. Before she could take two steps, he closed the door, hauled her in his arms and kissed her until she saw stars.

"Do you have any plans tonight?"

Leigh didn't know how he expected her to answer. He had every inch of her body awake and clamoring for more of his magnificent kisses. She finally managed to say, "No. Why?"

"Would you like to accompany me to a gathering? I'm sure there'll be poetry readings and art."

Miles knew she would never turn down an opportunity to view art. She loved it almost as much as singing and had purchased two paintings that she left behind. Anger bubbled up inside her when she thought about her favorite sculpture. She'd spent most of her savings on the Hiawatha bust sculpted by Edmonia Lewis. She'd been surprised to see it as part of an estate sale since many of her pieces had been lost. And Percy had stolen it. He'd asked her about its worth on one occasion and insinuated the money it brought in would be helpful in starting his church. She pointedly told him it was none of his business and not for sale. But on the visit to ostensibly ask her father for her hand, the sculpture had mysteriously disappeared. Pushing down the emotion, she smiled. "I'd love to go, but I don't have a fancy dress." Leigh hadn't been to any gatherings as a guest and had spent most of her money on clothes she needed for her job.

"I'm sure you'll look beautiful in anything you wear. It starts at eight, but I'd like to have dinner before with you beforehand, if that's all right."

"That would be fine."

"I'll pick you up at six." Miles took a step toward her and halted. "I'd better go. Your lips are calling me and if I stand here a minute longer, I'm going to answer. Then we'll miss the party."

The party was five hours away. Surely he didn't mean— His heated gaze and wicked grin let her know he meant exactly what she thought.

He chuckled. "I'll see you in a bit."

Leigh closed the door behind him. Memories of their one time together flooded her mind. She had been nervous and afraid, but because of his tender and gentle manner, she had enjoyed being with him. The powerful explosion that resulted had kept her body pulsing for hours. Her nipples tightened and she thought it best to set her thoughts elsewhere, like finding something appropriate to wear tonight.

She searched and settled on a mauve silk sleeveless drop waist dress. The neckline dipped slightly lower than what she typically wore, but fit with the current evening fashion, as did the scalloped hem.

When she opened the door to Miles later, Leigh had a bad case of nerves. This would be the first time she went out in public with a man. Their previous relationship had been done in secret and all Percy's visits had been at her parent's house, despite the fact that she'd had no interest in him. "Please come in." He looked even more handsome in the brown vested suit.

"You are stunning. I'll be the envy of every man tonight."

She picked her handbag and wrap. "Flattery?"

"Truth." Miles extended his arm. "Shall we?"

Leigh hooked her arm in his and let herself be escorted out. He stopped at a black Model T Ford and opened the door. "Whose car is this?"

"Mine."

Surprise filled her face. She didn't know many people who had cars. As he drove off, she asked, "When did you buy it?"

He gave her a sidelong glance. "About a year ago. I got tired of being put off the train or in having to ride in the cattle car."

She understood his thinking. The Jim Crow laws that divided the races was supposed to create a separate but equal standard of treatment, but there was nothing equal about having to ride with cattle. She had worried about that on her journey, but had been fortunate enough to have a conductor who seated passengers fairly. There were some Whites who frowned at her presence, but no one said anything. Blessedly, she'd made it to her destination without mishap.

They dined at a restaurant that served southern food reminiscent of her mother's and pangs of sadness surfaced for a short time. At the conclusion of the meal, she said, "You never told me who's having the party."

"It's a surprise," Miles said as they started on the next part of their night.

Leigh was definitely surprised when they entered the townhouse belonging to A'Lelia Walker, Madame C.J. Walker's daughter. The woman's hair care company had been very successful and A'Lelia had taken over her mother's business several years ago. Leigh finally had a chance to meet

A'Lelia, who stood almost six feet tall and wore a turban on her head. Miss Walker had transformed her salon into what she called The Dark Tower. There, Leigh had a chance to meet writers Langston Hughes and Zora Neale Hurston, who were part of the New Negro Movement, and promoted art as a way to uplift the race. Miles stayed by her side and saw to her every need and she had a wonderful time. He seemed to know the things that would bring her the most joy. First, the ice cream, and now, this. She enjoyed spending time with him and hoped he didn't break her heart again.

CHAPTER 5

Miles enjoyed seeing the excitement on Leigh's face. As he'd told her, he remembered everything about her. She stood talking to a small group of women and he admired her dress. The way it framed her curves had had him in a state of arousal since she opened the door to him. He told himself he needed to go slowly this time, let her get used to him being around, but he didn't know how much longer he could hold out. Leigh tempted him like no other woman. In reality, he shouldn't even be thinking about her in these terms. Even though times were changing for women, his Leigh didn't fit that category. She was still very much an innocent. He'd already succumbed to temptation once and was doing his best not to pressure her in any way. Yet, the sight of another man talking to her and smiling at her sent a sharp jolt of envy through his gut. Relief flooded him when she moved to speak with a group of women.

"Miles Cooper."

He faced the man who'd called out his name, a musician he had met a few weeks ago. "How are you, Issac?"

"Doing well. I caught the show over at the Magnolia Club. That Leigh Jones sure can sing. She's a beautiful woman."

"That she is."

"A woman like that...I wouldn't mind taking the long way around—"

Miles's glare stopped Issac midsentence. Rather than knocking the man out like he wanted to, he decided it was time for him to move on, but not before issuing a warning. "Don't ever let me hear you talking about Leigh so disrespectfully again," he said through clenched teeth. "And stay the hell away from her. Are we clear?" Isaac tried to show some bravado, but with Miles towering over him, thought better about it.

"Real clear," he answered tightly.

"Good." Miles left the man standing there. He joined Leigh. "Excuse me, ladies. Leigh may I speak with you?"

"Yes." Leigh smiled at the women and thanked them for the conversation.

Miles inclined his head and escorted Leigh away. He knew the party would probably last until the wee hours of the morning, but he wanted to leave and spend some time alone with her. "Are you enjoying yourself?"

"I am, very much. Thank you for this, Miles. It's getting late, so we should probably say our farewells."

"Then we'll do that." They said goodbye to those around them, found their hostess, thanked her and departed.

On the drive home, Leigh said, "I can't believe I had a chance to meet all the people I've read so much about. How did you manage to get an invitation?"

"I met Taylor Gordon a couple of weeks ago. Miss Walker is a big supporter. He's done some theater."

"That's nice. Do you think the race will ever be treated fairly?"

"I don't know. But my grandmother seems to think that one day we'll be going to the same schools as Whites and running large companies."

"That would be something."

He thought the same, but didn't believe he would see it in his lifetime. Maybe his children would. Miles went still. Where had that thought come from? He'd never contemplated having children, or taking a wife, for that matter. He didn't know anything about being a husband or father, but realized the life he had growing up wasn't something he wanted any potential children he might have to experience. He often imagined what his life would have been like had his mother lived. The few times his father had spoken of her gave Miles the impression that she had been a gentle and loving woman. Under her guidance, Miles might have learned how to show love.

His father rarely showed emotion, but Miles knew the old man loved him and did the best he could with the hand he had been dealt, and traveled as a way of keeping his grief at bay. Subsequently, Miles hadn't spent much time in school. However, whenever they visited Mama, she made sure he kept up with his lessons. He envied that about Leigh. She'd even gone to college and become a teacher. And with her sweet personality, he was sure the students loved her. Had she regretted leaving them? "Do you miss teaching?"

A soft smile curved Leigh's lips. "Not really. Though I do miss the students, sometimes. Becoming a teacher had never been my dream. It was what my father wanted me to do. He had to quit school when he was young to help his parents work their farm. He always said that in order for the race to improve, we need good teachers. I agree, but I just didn't want to be one of them," she added softly.

"You must miss your parents." Miles couldn't imagine how hard it must be living on her own so far away from home, especially since girls were raised to believe that their futures included a husband and children.

"I do."

He gave her hand a gentle squeeze. "But I'm sure they're glad to know you're doing well."

She didn't comment, but stared out the window.

"Leigh?"

Shifting in her seat to face him, she said, "My parents don't know where I am. I never told them. Can you believe I actually just posted the first letter to them today?"

He frowned. She had been in New York for the past three years with no one but Liz? What if something happened? All this time, he assumed she'd been corresponding with her family. The knowledge that she hadn't did not sit well with him and made him feel even worse for leaving her the way he had. "Why didn't you write to them?"

"Guilt mostly. In the note I left, I only said that was going to pursue my dreams and hoped that they would forgive me someday."

Miles didn't know she was crying until he saw her wipe away a tear. "I'm sorry. At least you've done it now. That counts for something."

"I hope so."

They rode the rest of the way in silence. Miles walked her to the door and knew he should leave, but he couldn't get his feet to cooperate. Instead, he simply observed her, trying to discern why this particular woman affected him so.

Leigh placed her handbag and wrap on an end table and faced him. "Whatever is the matter?"

"Do you have any idea how smart and beautiful I think you are?" Miles crossed the floor to where she stood and used his finger to trace a path across the tops of her breasts visible above the dress. "Tonight as I watched you, I had a hard time not dragging you off to the nearest closet and showing you just what you do to me."

She gasped softly.

He bent and replaced his finger with his tongue. A low moan escaped her lips and the sound aroused him further. He reached behind her, unzipped the dress and let it pool at her waist. He tugged down her camisole and fully exposed the breasts he knew fit perfectly in his hands. Miles circled his tongue around one dark nipple, and then the other before drawing it into his mouth and sucking gently.

"We shouldn't be…ohh."

Her knees buckled and Miles held her tightly to keep her from falling. He swept her into his arms, carried her to the sofa and sat with her across his lap. He continued to reacquaint himself with the taste and feel of her. Her uninhibited responses had him on the brink of losing control and he needed to slow down. Gifting her with one more kiss, he lifted his head. She made such a sensual picture lying in his arms he had to close his eyes. He was as hard as a steel beam and he drew in several calming breaths. To keep from taking her fully, he sat her next to him and got up to put some distance between them.

"What are you doing?" Leigh walked over, pulled his head down and kissed him with a passion that stunned him. "Why did you stop?"

Miles groaned and set her away. "Things are about to get out of hand and we need to slow down, sweetheart." He righted her clothes. "I'm trying to be good, but you're making it very difficult."

"You were being good," she countered, wrapping her arms around him.

He laughed softly and pulled her closer. "You are something else." Knowing that she wanted him as much as he did her told him he had to leave. *Now.* He kissed the top of her head. "I have to go. Otherwise, we'll end up doing something we aren't ready for."

"You're probably right. But I did enjoy your kisses."

He enjoyed hers, too. So much so that it would take hours for his body to calm down. At the moment, he could use a bottle of that whiskey Liz served. "Good night. I'll see you in the morning at rehearsal." Unable to resist, he kissed her again. "One more…"

When he got home, he was too wound up to sleep. Instead, he sat at the table and wrote music. The same melody that had been playing in his head for the past three years floated around, but he had yet to write it down. There seemed to be a crucial part missing, one he couldn't figure out. But it would come to him. It always did. An hour later, he had composed a jazz tune he planned to present to the band tomorrow. He had no idea whether they'd be open to it, with him being new, but the song was perfect for Leigh's voice.

Miles leaned back in the chair. Leigh. His groin stirred just thinking about her. Slow was not going to work much longer.

* * *

Leigh lay in bed Friday morning staring at the ceiling and thinking about Miles. She couldn't get his kisses out of her mind and her body had been in a state of turmoil since he left last night. He always made her feel things society said weren't proper for a lady, but she didn't want to settle for a man who aroused nothing more than polite conversation. She remembered catching her parents sharing a kiss more than once and seeing her father whisper something to her mother that had the woman giggling like a schoolgirl. She wanted what her grandparents and parents had—that special person who could make her heart beat faster just by walking in the room. All the things she shared with Miles. Leigh had agreed to give him another chance and, so far, he had been as attentive as any woman could want. But for how long? That was the crux of her problem. He'd said he didn't plan to leave again, but hadn't offered anything in the way of commitment.

She glanced over at the clock. She still had a couple of hours before rehearsal. Maybe a talk with Liz would help. Leigh threw back the covers, dressed and ate a quick breakfast. She wanted to catch her friend before she headed down to start her day. Thirty minutes later, she walked to the other end of the hall and knocked on Liz's apartment door. No answer. She took the stairs down and froze at the sight of a man placing bottles of whiskey in what looked like a false space behind the bar.

"That'll do it, Miss Liz," she heard the man say. "I'll bring your next order in a couple of weeks."

Leigh stepped back and brought her hand to her mouth. *A bootlegger?*

"Thanks, Mack."

"You know I'm still waiting on you, woman."

Leigh's eyes widened as the man sidled up to Liz and kissed her.

Liz giggled. "Mmm hmm. I'm sure you tell that to all the girls."

"Now that's where you're wrong. I don't play with *girls*. You're the only woman I want, Elizabeth. I'll see you on Sunday night. Keep yourself safe."

"You do the same."

Leigh waited until she heard the side door close before making her presence known. "Well, now. Seems like I'm not the only one keeping secrets."

Liz jumped and spun around. "Leigh! Girl, you almost gave me heart failure. What are you talking about?"

She sauntered over to the bar. "*Mack.*" Liz's mouth fell open. "He's a bootlegger, for heaven's sake. He could be dangerous."

"That man is only dangerous to my heart."

"What if the police raid the club?"

"You just mind the stage and I'll take care of everything else," she said pointedly. "And why are you down here spying on me this early?"

Leigh smiled. "I wasn't spying. I came to talk to you, but you were sort of occupied. Actually, you still look a little woozy."

Liz tried to glare, but they both burst out laughing. "Shut up." Once they calmed, she asked, "What did you want to talk about?"

"Miles. We're...he's..."

"Courting you? Everybody knows that, honey. You still think he'll be leaving again?" She added water and coffee grounds to a percolator coffee pot and plugged it in.

"I don't know. But that's not the problem."

"Well, what is the problem?" Leigh was quiet for so long, Liz said, "I can't read your mind so you're going to have to help me out."

"Men and women things," she finally blurted.

She studied her a long moment. "I see."

"I figured since you were married before, you'd know if I'm crazy or not."

Liz snorted. "Evan was a nice man, but he believed what most men do, that sex is only for them." Her husband had died less than a year into the marriage from an illness. "Don't get me wrong, he was respectful and tender in bed, but there was no heat. I assume you're asking me these questions because you believe this is where you and Miles are headed."

Leigh dropped her head guiltily. She and Miles were way past that point. "It was only once and..."

She covered Leigh's hand. "I'm not judging. The only thing that matters is how *you* feel. Are you worried because you didn't like it?"

62

Leigh shook her head.

"Then that means he made you feel like you'd been flung to the stars," Liz said with a laugh. "I can tell by just looking at that man he knows his way around a woman's body. Mmm hmm, yes, ma'am!"

"You are a mess, girl. What about Mack?"

"He hits me the same way. Showed me how fun and passionate it could be and all that I'd missed with Evan." A soft smile curved her lips, as if she were remembering one of those moments. "Anyway, this isn't about me. If you liked it, why are you worried?"

"What if he leaves again? Sleeping with him will only complicate things more." They had grown closer than before over the past month and Leigh had fallen harder. She couldn't take him leaving a second time.

Liz sighed. "I don't know. Did he ever tell you why he left the first time?"

"No." Somehow, she hadn't gotten around to asking again, but she needed those answers in order to move forward with their relationship. "He only said it had nothing to do with me, but I need to know why."

She got two cups, poured the coffee and slid one across to Leigh. "Do you think it had to do with another woman?"

Leigh added sugar to her cup and stirred. "I have no idea, but I admit it was the first thing that crossed my mind three years ago. That somewhere he had a wife he had to get back to." Even now, the thought made her stomach turn.

"Somehow, I can't see that."

She hoped not. She blew on her coffee and sipped carefully while continuing the conversation. They finished their coffee and Leigh went back upstairs to get ready for rehearsal.

When she came back, Miles was sitting at the piano playing what sounded like a slow blues tune. He stopped and glanced up at her approach. "You don't have to stop. I've never heard that one before."

"It's not finished yet. Just something that's been playing around in my head. Good morning. How did you sleep?"

Leigh smiled. "Good morning. Quite well," she lied.

"That makes one of us," Miles cracked, and started another melody. "I laid in bed thinking about your kisses all night. How about you?"

She stared.

His hands paused over the keys and he met her gaze. "We're going to have to handle this soon."

She sighed inwardly. "I know." Thankfully, at that moment, Loyce entered. Miles gave her a look that said the conversation wasn't over.

The rehearsal went well, but Leigh wanted to sing something new and asked about it.

Willie shrugged. "Frank wrote most of the songs for the band. Me, Sam and Loyce just left it to him."

"Actually," Miles started, "I wrote a song I'd like you all to take a look at." He handed music sheets to the three men and to Leigh, making sure to brush his hands across hers.

Leigh tried to ignore the contact and focus on the papers. After a few minutes of perusal, Willie and Loyce began playing bars on their respective instruments. Sam waded in on drums.

"This ain't bad, Miles. Ain't bad at all," Loyce said.

"Thanks. I think Miss Leigh will do it proud."

She scanned the lyrics of the song titled, In My Dreams and eyed Miles. The song was about a woman who struck out on her own to pursue her dreams with no plans to wait for a man, though she wouldn't mind having one around to keep her warm at night. "Let me hear the music."

Miles played the up-tempo piece staring directly into her eyes without missing a beat. "What do you think?" he asked when the song ended.

Leigh grudgingly admitted that it would be perfect for their audience. She could already feel the melody coursing through her. "I like it." She also realized it wasn't the same song he'd been playing when she entered, but didn't want to ask about it in front of the other two men since Miles didn't mention it as being one of the songs for the band.

He chuckled. "I knew you would. Think you can be ready to sing it tomorrow night?"

Saturdays were their biggest nights and, lately, Liz had been teasing about needing to expand the place even more. "Sure." Instead of ending practice, they continued for another hour, with plans to rehearse in the morning and packed up just as the restaurant opened.

Leigh waited until the other band members left to ask about the other song. "Are you going to let the band hear the other song you were playing? It was very nice, too."

Miles stood from the piano. "Care to join me for lunch?"

"So you aren't going to answer my question?"

He lifted a brow. "You didn't answer mine, either."

"Fine. Let's get a table." She spun on her heel and headed toward the hostess station.

He laughed softly and followed. Once they were seated, he said, "No."

Leigh looked up from her menu, confused. "No, what?"

"I'm answering your question."

"Why not? It would be great."

The conversation paused while the server took their order. Then Miles said, "It's not finished and I don't know if it ever will be, so…" He shrugged. "There are a few things that aren't finished between us either, but I'm sure they'll settle themselves in time."

Her pulse skipped.

He leaned forward and trained his midnight gaze on her. "I dreamed of being here with you like this for three long years and there's no comparison to the real thing."

Leigh almost fainted. Something told her that she was in danger of losing her heart to him once more.

CHAPTER 6

Leigh could barely get through the night's performance for thinking about Mile's words. They seemed to whisper across the stage every time he glanced her way. By the end of the first set, she needed more than water to cool her down. She stood against the door of her dressing room and took several deep, calming breaths. She wasn't one for drinking spirits, but she seriously considered going over to the bar and asking for a glass of whatever Mack and Liz had hidden behind the wall. A knock startled her.

"Are you okay, Leigh?"

She opened the door to Miles. "I'm fine. Why?"

"You left rather quickly and I wanted to make sure everything was alright."

She waved a hand. "Oh, it was just really hot. I can't believe how many people are here tonight."

Miles smiled knowingly. "Mmm hmm." He tilted her chin and placed a sweet kiss on her lips. "See you in a minute."

Leigh nodded.

He gave her that patented grin and walked off.

She closed the door again. How could one man make her melt so easily? Every heated glance and subtle touch brought her closer to the edge of losing control. If she did, her only problem would be not wanting him to stop. Ever.

Ten minutes later, Leigh went back on stage in control and determined not to let Miles and his seductive smile rattle her. She did well until the last song. Somehow, her original closing song, Tain't Nobody's Business If I Do, had been replaced by their duet. Though he kept his distance, when he sang the verse promising his woman that he wouldn't tarry and leave her all alone, that he would come just as fast as his legs could carry him and love her all night long, she was lost.

While the audience clapped, hooted and whistled, Leigh did well to keep her smile in place.

Miles materialized next to her and raised a hand to silence the crowd. "Let's give one more round of applause for Miss Leigh." He waited a moment until the resulting response died down. "If you think tonight was something, you don't want to miss out tomorrow. We'll have a brand new tune and you can only hear it at The Magnolia Club."

Leigh whipped her head in his direction. If the buzz generated by his announcement was any indication, Liz would probably need to knock out that wall by morning. As the crowd filtered out, she heard several people making plans to come early to make sure they had a seat.

Liz rushed over to where Leigh, Miles and Loyce stood talking. She had a huge smile on her face. "Miles, you sure are good for business."

"Miss Liz, I have to agree," Loyce said. "You might want to keep him on."

Leigh divided a speculative glance between Loyce and Liz. "What about Frank? I thought he was getting better?"

Loyce nodded. "He is, but it's going to be best if he just moves on or goes back home to Chicago where his family lives." He shrugged. "Maybe he can find some piano work there. As long as he keeps his nose clean."

"Those men aren't going to let him be until they have their money or his life," Liz added. "I'd rather him keep his life. Loyce and I saw him off on the train this morning and I gave him a nice settlement."

Leigh squeezed her friend's hand. "That was very kind, Liz." She just wished she had been able to say goodbye.

"Well, you all go on home, so that I can get some rest. I have a feeling I'm going to need to pay a visit to the funeral parlor to rent some chairs for tomorrow."

They all laughed and said their goodbyes.

"I'll be up in about five minutes," Miles whispered as he passed her.

The discussion about Frank had made her momentarily forget about what might take place. She gave him a barely perceptible nod and made her way to her apartment.

Upstairs, Leigh paced the length of her small front room, not knowing whether to change clothes, put up a pot of tea or what. A knock on the door settled the matter. She slowly walked over and opened it and stepped back for Miles to enter. She didn't know what she expected to happen next—he'd kiss her, they'd go to the bedroom—but it wasn't him walking her over to the sofa, draping her legs across his lap, taking off her shoes and massaging her feet. The pressure of his hands extinguished the aches that always accompanied the long hours on stage.

"I don't know how you do it, night after night, in these heels. These beautiful, brown legs look good, but I know they're tired." Miles lifted one leg, placed a lingering kiss there and repeated the action on the other before continuing his ministrations.

The kneading felt so good Leigh could only manage a soft moan. His hands moved higher, pushing her dress further up to expose her thighs. "This feels so good, Miles," she murmured. Her head fell back against the sofa and her eyes closed.

"That's what I want—to make you feel good." His hands slid up her outer thighs and grasped her hips.

Leigh's eyes opened and held his for a long moment.

69

Miles stilled. Keeping his eyes locked on hers, he said, "We'll only go as far as you want, baby. Anytime you want me to stop, for any reason, just say so."

Stopping was the furthest thing from her mind. "Don't stop." He resumed his quest. Warmth spread through her veins. Her breasts tingled and her core throbbed and pulsed. As if he knew just what she needed, Miles's fingers went to the space between her legs. He circled the bud, teasing. Moans spilled from her lips as the sensations brought on by his touch intensified. Her breath stacked up in her throat and a moment later, she shattered like a pane of glass. Leigh buried her face in the sofa to keep from screaming loud enough to wake the neighbors. While her body still trembled, Miles lifted her into his strong arms and carried her down the short hallway to her bedroom. She took a moment to turn on the lamp by her bed. He slowly and sensually stripped away all of her clothing, then kissed his way down her body. His hands roamed across her belly, over her hips and down her thighs. Miles captured her mouth in a slow-as-molasses kiss. His tongue made sweeping, swirling motions in her mouth and a flurry of sensations raced through her.

"You are more beautiful than I remember," Miles said as his heated gaze roamed down her body. He stood and undressed.

Leigh couldn't take her eyes off his well-defined chest and abs. The muscles of his arms and legs rippled with every movement. "And you're more handsome than I remember."

A slight grin tilted the corner of his mouth. Miles sheathed himself in the rubber and lowered himself next to Leigh on the bed. He lowered his head and touched his mouth to hers. "I missed you, Leigh. More than you'll ever know."

He stared at her as if he wanted to say more, but didn't. The kisses started again and he trailed a series down her jaw and neck to the valley between her breasts. He took one hardened nipple between his lips and sucked gently. "Oh, Miles." His hand found her center again and he slid one long finger inside. "*Yesss,*" she moaned as his skillful fingers continued their magic. He added another one and her body splintered again. Leigh let out a keening cry.

"How do you feel now, sweetheart? Still good?"

She couldn't even begin to answer him with her body in the throes of such pleasure. He moved his body over hers and she tensed slightly as he pushed at her entrance. It must have shown on her face.

Miles's brow lifted. "Are you okay? It's like —"

"Yes. It's just that…there's been no one else, but you."

A look of tenderness washed over his face. "Then we'll go slow, just like the first time."

He teased her with short strokes, moving in and out until she was comfortable. The flame rose again and Leigh remembered why she had enjoyed herself. Her hands glided over his firm back muscles and she lifted her hips to meet each of his well-placed thrusts. He angled her higher and increased the pace, setting her whole being on fire. This time the orgasm started somewhere around her belly and flared out to the rest of her body and she erupted with a force that made her almost pass out. Waves of sensation washed over her.

Miles plunged deeper and brought her in for a spine-tingling kiss. He abruptly tore his mouth away, buried his head in her neck and found his own release. He let out a low moan, his sounds of pleasure mingling with hers. "Leigh. Sweet, sweet, Leigh," he called almost reverently. He caressed her face then kissed her softly.

When he withdrew and wrapped her in his arms, she wished it could always be this way between them. If he left again… She closed her arms and snuggled closer.

They lay in silence a long while. "What are you thinking about?"

"How do you know I'm thinking?"

"I know you. That mind never stops going."

She wanted to ask if he planned to stay, but was afraid of the answer. Instead, she asked, "Why did you leave me?"

His deep sigh ruffled the silence. "I do owe you an explanation." Another minute passed before he started speaking. "My mother died when I was three and it devastated my father. My grandmother, his mother, tried to get him to stay with her in Louisiana, but he was so brokenhearted that he packed me up and took to the road. He could play that piano—much better than I do—so he always had a gig somewhere. We never stayed in one place for more than two or three months, but wherever we went, he managed to keep a roof over our heads and food on the table. I remember sometimes walking for hours to the next town and being happy when someone came along in a buggy to give us a ride, especially during the summer heat or winter freeze. It wasn't an easy life, but he was my pa and I didn't mind, as long as we were together."

Leigh's heart broke for the life he'd had to lead. She could hear the deep affection he felt for his father, but it still didn't answer her question.

"Anyway, that was my life until he died in the war. After that, I tried to go back to Louisiana with Mama, get a farm job, but I couldn't stay. A few months later, I hit the road again. But when I met you, something inside me wanted to stay." Miles propped up on an elbow and peered down at her. "The first time I heard your voice, I was a goner. But that's not what captured me."

"No?"

He shook his head. "This." He placed his hand on her heart. "This is what held my attention—your amazing heart and giving spirit. I told you that back in Magnolia. I've never met anyone else like you. I didn't want to leave you, Leigh, believe me, but I didn't know how to stay."

Leigh placed her hand against his cheek. "Your father would be proud of you. You've kept yourself out of trouble and, as far as playing the piano, I don't know anybody better than you. But what about now, Miles? I don't want to wake up one morning and find you gone again."

"That's what I've been trying to tell you. I'm ready to put down roots, Leigh. No matter where I went, you were never far from my mind. Or my heart." He wiped away her tears. "Don't cry. I mean it this time. I'm here to stay."

She searched his face for any hint of guile, but saw only sincerity. The wall around her heart dropped a little further. "Okay." They shared a smile and Miles placed a tender kiss on her lips. "Where did you go after you left Magnolia?"

"Everywhere—Chicago, New Orleans, Kansas, California."

"You traveled all the way to California?"

"Yep, and I picked up something for you while I was in San Francisco."

She sat up. "What is it?"

Miles chuckled. "I'll bring it tomorrow and you can see for yourself."

"Why haven't you given it to me before now?"

He shrugged. "Don't know. Just never felt the time was right. But I do now." He traced a finger over her lips and kissed her. He lay back on the pillow and held her for a while longer. "Speaking of tomorrow, I should go."

Leigh would have loved for him to hold her all night, but knew they had no choice. "I know." As he left the bed, she scanned his naked body from head to toe and smiled. It reminded her of one of those nude sculptures she'd seen with every muscle drawn to perfection. He dressed without a word. She slid off the bed and put on her robe.

Miles took her hand and led her to the front. "Get some rest, baby. I'll see you tomorrow." He kissed her deeply once more and rested his forehead against hers. "Lock up." He opened the door, stuck his head out to make sure no one was there and stepped out.

"Be careful, Miles," Leigh whispered. He nodded and loped down the hall toward the stairs. She waited until he disappeared around the corner before closing the door. With times being the way they were, the night could be especially dangerous and she didn't want anything to happen to him. Not when she was falling in love with him again.

* * *

Despite only a couple hours of sleep, Miles felt more energized than he had in a long time. He couldn't stop thinking about what he'd shared with Leigh. Even now, the melody of her passionate cries played in his head...and his heart. He finally understood why he missed her so much, why he had to come back. He loved her. And he finally had the missing piece to the song he'd been working on for three years. It didn't fit the current jazz or blues sound, but he instinctively knew with Leigh's voice, it could be a bestselling race record. Back in Magnolia, she had confided in him that her ultimate dream was to see her name on a record. He planned to make it happen.

Miles removed the box he kept tucked safely in his suitcase and opened it. He carefully unwrapped the paper and inspected it for damage. When he had seen the sculpture in an art studio while in San Francisco, he knew he had to buy it for Leigh. He had been pleasantly surprised that the owner was a woman of the race. Maybe once he saved up a bit more money, he and Leigh could train out to California to purchase something else. Miles rewrapped the sculpture, placed it back in the box and put it into his satchel. He made sure he had everything, then headed over to the Magnolia. He couldn't wait to see Leigh's face.

It was going to be hard not to haul her into his arms and kiss her the moment he saw her, but he preferred to keep all their dealings private for the time being. As he drove, he debated on whether to tell her that he loved her. It would go a long way in showing her that he meant what he said about staying around, but what if she didn't feel the same? By the time he entered the club, he had decided to keep his feelings to himself for now. It would give him more time to court her and show her that this time would be for keeps.

Chapter 7

"Your head in the clouds, Leigh?"

Leigh glanced over at Miles and they shared a secret smile. She'd had a hard time keeping focus during the rehearsal. Every time she looked Miles's way, she found him staring at her with barely veiled heat in his eyes. "Just thinking about what Willie is saying." He had suggested changing around the music set to keep the audience guessing.

"They would expect us to do the new song first, most likely. But if we put it somewhere in the middle or near the end, it would guarantee them staying for the whole show," Loyce said.

Sam laughed. "Now, Loyce, you know them folks ain't leaving 'til the last note leaves Miss Leigh's mouth. It doesn't matter where we put the new song."

Miles chuckled. "Sam has a point, but I vote for putting it at the end. It'll be a nice build-up." He rotated toward Leigh. "Leigh?"

She shrugged. "It doesn't matter to me. You all start playing and I'll start singing." After another minute of discussion, they decided to put it at the end. Leigh's attention shifted to the noise behind her. Liz was directing her staff in rearranging the restaurant. Tables had been moved, a few more added and stacks of folding chairs were propped against the wall. "I guess Liz was serious."

"And with the sixty-cent cover charge, she's going to make a fortune tonight," Loyce cracked. They all laughed. "Well, I'm going to head out. Think I want to go find a new suit for tonight."

"Is there a certain young lady you're interested in courting, Loyce?" Leigh teased. She'd seen him talking to a woman after the show for the past week.

He grinned sheepishly. "Her name's Delores."

"Well, I wish you and Delores all the best."

"Thanks, Miss Leigh."

Leigh smiled. After Sam, Loyce and Willie left, she turned and found Miles watching her again. "What?"

"So, if there was a certain young lady I was interested in courting, would you wish me the best, too?"

"Depends on if you promised to be true and do your best not to leave her in pieces."

He rose from the piano bench and came toward her. "Then it shouldn't be a problem because she's the only woman I want and I promise to be true and never, ever leave her in pieces."

Oh my! The heat arched between them. Leigh brought her hand to her chest, hoping to calm her runaway heartbeat.

Miles lifted his hand toward her face, and then as if remembering where they were, quickly dropped it. "Come upstairs with me, so I can give you your gift."

Still trying to process his earlier statement, she nodded. Since it was day, she didn't see a problem with letting him come up for a few minutes.

"I'll go around back."

"No, it's okay."

He studied her a moment. "Are you sure?"

"Yes." He followed her upstairs and she waited while he extracted something from his bag.

Miles handed her the elongated box. "I found this in San Francisco a few months ago. I thought you might like it."

Leigh opened the box and carefully unwrapped the paper. She gasped. "Oh, Miles. This is absolutely *beautiful*."

Mesmerized, she ran her hand over the sculpture of a couple in a passionate embrace. The faces had been sculpted with such detail she could feel their emotion. Their features were without a doubt Negro. "The artist was someone of the race?"

He smiled. "Yes. A real nice lady named Ava Lydell. Should be a card in the box with her information."

She dug through the wrapping and found a small card with the artist's name, studio name — Art by Ava — and address in San Francisco. "I have to send her a thank you note to let her know how much I love it." She ran her hand over the piece again. "I can't get over how lovely this is." She set it on the table and wrapped her arms around Miles's waist. Tears misted her eyes. "I don't know how I'll ever thank you. This is the most amazing gift I've ever received."

"If I could've bought the whole studio, I would have just to see your smile. Maybe we can train out to California and visit the studio before winter."

In that moment, Leigh fell a little more. She came up on tiptoe and kissed him, infusing it with all the gratitude and love she felt in her heart. "I don't need you to buy me the whole studio. You make me smile just by being you. You always seem to know the things that make me happiest. And I'd love to visit the studio with you."

Miles cradled her face in his hands. "I told you before, I want to be the only man to make you smile, to give you the desires of your heart, to court you."

This time when he kissed her, she felt everything he was telling her clear to her toes. The emotions overwhelmed her so much she broke off the kiss. Leigh rested her head against his chest. The strong, rapid pace of his heart matched her own. Miles lightly ran his hand up and down her spine.

At length, he stepped back. "I'm going to go so you can rest up for tonight." He paused. "How are you feeling?" At her confused look, he said, "Last night."

Understanding dawned. "I'm fine. A little sore, but not in a bad way."

"I'm glad." He stood there a minute longer. "I'm really trying to leave, but those lips keep calling me."

Leigh laughed and pushed him toward the door. "No more kisses for you, Mr. Cooper." But contrary to her words, she pulled his head down for a kiss that left them both breathing hard. "That should hold you until later," she said with a smile.

"Yes, ma'am. I do believe I can make it until tonight. See you later, sweetheart."

"Bye, Miles and thank you, again, for the beautiful sculpture."

"You're welcome." Miles tossed her a bold wink and left.

Still smiling, she walked back over to the table and fingered the figurine. She couldn't believe he had given her such a precious gift. She saw the card and recalled that she wanted to send a note to Miss Lydell. Grabbing some stationery from her bedroom, Leigh composed a short letter and put in an envelope. She would take it to the post office on Monday. She stared at the sculpture and wondered what made Miles chose this particular piece. A memory surfaced in her mind of the picnic she and Miles had snuck of to have three years ago. At the end of the day, she hadn't wanted to leave and he stood holding and kissing her by the lake in an embrace much like this couple. Had he been thinking of them? The next time they had a moment, she'd ask. She yawned. Maybe a nap was in order. Afterward she would make a quick run to the dress shop for a new pair of stockings.

Obviously Leigh was more tired than she realized because when she woke up, she only had an hour to get ready. She reheated some of the stew she'd made, added a small piece of cornbread and lemonade and quickly ate. Thankfully, she found a pair of stockings in good shape and dressed in record time. Leigh put the signature Magnolia flower in her hair and hurried downstairs.

She poked her head in the door from the hallway and could only stare. People crowded at every table, chair and barstool, and not one ounce of floor space could be seen.

Liz sidled next to her. "Girl, will you look at this. You know I'm never letting you leave here, right?" she added with a laugh.

Leigh shook her head and smiled. "I owe you. I'll be here as long as you want. This is something, though."

"That Miles is a genius. How are you two getting along?"

Heat filled her face and she averted her eyes.

"That well, huh? Well, at least you're both rowing in the same direction now. Yes?"

"Yes. I...he's special. He purchased a sculpture for me while he was in San Francisco."

Liz's eyes widened. "To replace the one Percy stole?"

"No. He doesn't know about that, or Percy. He said he saw it and thought I'd like it. It's *incredible*. I'll have to show you tomorrow." The announcer's voice filtered through. "That's my cue."

She squeezed Leigh's hand. "I am so proud of you."

"Thanks." The two women embraced and Leigh went on stage.

By the time they reached the end of the set, Leigh could sense the anticipation in the audience. "We thank you for coming and I know you're all waiting for our new song. Well, the wait is over. Ladies and gentlemen, In My Dreams. Though I'm going to sing it, the credit goes to Miles Cooper, who wrote the music and the lyrics." She waved in Mile's direction and he tipped his hat. She nodded to the band. It didn't take long for the audience to get into the song, clapping and swaying in their seats. The words of the song resonated with Leigh so much that it was easy for her to become one with the music. She belted out the lyrics about not letting anything stop you from pursuing your dreams with such conviction, at the end she heard a man yell out, "I know you're going to be my dream, Miss Leigh!"

The song had the same reaction during the second set and she couldn't have been happier. She caught Miles's gaze and he smiled. She smiled back. Yes, they were definitely rowing in the same direction.

* * *

Sunday morning, Miles sat at the kitchen table sipping his coffee and thinking about how well things went last night. His heart had nearly beaten out of his chest with pride when Leigh sang his song. He'd known it would be perfect for her and she had surpassed his greatest expectations. As he left The Magnolia, Liz had asked whether he'd thought about approaching one of the recording companies about the song, and suggested he should. He'd think about it at some point, but he had better song he wanted to pitch. First he had to share it with Leigh because it would only work if she agreed to sing it with him.

Miles took another sip of coffee and scanned the music sheets spread out in front of him. The untitled music was complete. He just needed the lyrics, and once they came, the title would, too. He leaned back in the chair and let the words fill his mind. Immediately Leigh's face appeared and he was transported back to Friday night—the way she touched him, the way she kissed him and the sound of her passionate cries while they made love. This was their love song, the beautiful music they created together. His eyes snapped open. Miles picked up the fountain pen and scribbled furiously, the words pouring from his brain so fast he could barely keep up. At length, he stopped and read over what he'd wrote, making small changes here and there. "This is it."

Anxious to hear it, Miles gathered up everything and hurried down to The Magnolia. The restaurant and club were closed today, but Liz had given him permission to come and practice whenever he wanted. He knocked on her apartment.

"Miles?" Liz stared, clearly surprised to see him. "Is something wrong?"

"Good morning, Miss Liz. Everything's fine. I just wanted to use the piano."

She visibly relaxed and smiled. "It's only ten. I figured you'd be sleeping in after last night. Working on another song for the band?"

"Something like that." He didn't like lying to her since she paid his salary, but this song was only for him and Leigh. He'd play it there first, but only two instruments were required—the piano and their voices.

"Be my guest. I have some of my staff coming in around three this afternoon to move the tables back. Will that bother you?"

"No, ma'am. If I'm done before that time, I'll let you know."

She nodded. "I'd appreciate that. Thank you."

Miles tipped his hat and took the stairs leading to the club. He settled at the piano and started playing. In no time, he lost himself in the music. The melody seeped into his soul as he sang the lyrics. He opened his eyes and his fingers stilled on the keys. "Leigh."

"Please don't stop playing. It's so beautiful."

His fingers moved over the keys as he sang the words into her eyes. "Every day when the sun rises, your voice is the first thing on my mind. It's the music of my heart, a rare and precious find. A beautiful melody sung one note at a time, creating our own love's serenade." Leigh came to where he sat, cupped his jaw and covered his mouth in a kiss so sweet it nearly stole his breath. Music forgotten, he pulled her down onto his lap and continued to kiss her.

"That's the song you were playing last week, the one you said wasn't finished."

"Yes."

"When did you finish it?"

"I finished the music Friday night and the words this morning."

"Friday?"

"After." Miles saw the moment she understood. "The melody has been in my head for three years, but I could never finish it because something was missing."

Leigh studied him. "Obviously you figured it out."

"Only after we made love. You were the missing piece." He hadn't planned on telling her about the song just yet, not until he felt it was perfect, but now that she'd heard it, he decided to share his plans. "Leigh, remember when you told me you dreamed of having your music on a record?"

"Yes." She smiled. "You told me you wanted the same thing."

"I did. I think this song might be our chance. What do you think?"

Her eyes widened and she brought her hand to her mouth. "Are you talking about taking the song to a record company?"

Miles grinned. "Yes. But I want to make sure you're okay with it. We'll have to practice and be damn near perfect, but I think we can pull it off."

Leigh threw her arms around him and squealed with delight. "Oh, my goodness!" She leaned back, her dark brown eyes sparkling. "Let's do it."

He loved her fearless spirit. He kissed her temple and patted her on the butt. "Up with you, woman. We've got work to do." Sharing a smile, Miles flew over the keys as they practiced the song for the next two hours.

When the last note faded away, Leigh asked, "Earlier, you said I was the missing piece to this song. What did you mean?"

"Exactly that. Bits and pieces of the song started in my head not long after I left you in Magnolia, but I could never figure out why I couldn't complete it. Until I saw you again. More and more of the music fell into place, but the full song only came the night we made love. Every touch, every kiss, every sound became this amazing melody and inspired the words."

"I don't know what to say. You inspire me, too," she added softly.

"That was one of the reasons I took the music when I left. I felt it." They fell silent for a moment.

"Do you think we can really do this?"

He heard the uncertainty in her voice. "I do."

Leigh angled her head thoughtfully. "It doesn't fit the current jazz or blues sound, though the slower tempo is closer to the blues."

"I know, but we don't want to sound like anybody else. I want you to stand out and be remembered forever."

"I want the same for you."

They sealed the deal with a long kiss. "What are you doing today?"

"Just relaxing, why?"

"Would you like to have dinner with me?"

"Most places are closed today."

"I know. I'm going to cook for you." Miles didn't know where those words came from. He'd never offered to cook for a woman, or anyone for that matter. He could make a decent meal—he'd had to learn to cook or starve—but he didn't do fancy.

Surprise lit her eyes. "I'd love to."

"Great. I'll come and pick you up around four. Is that okay?"

"It's perfect."

Miles sighed inwardly. Now what the hell was he going to cook? He walked Leigh up to her apartment, let Liz know he was leaving and prayed he had what he needed for dinner fixings.

After a thorough search, he settled on fried chicken, green beans with cut up potatoes and cornbread, all of which he could make reasonably well since it was one of his favorite meals. The two hours he had would be plenty of time to get everything done. He went about the task efficiently and had his grandmother to thank for his kitchen skills. Whenever Miles and his father stopped in to see her, she not only made sure he kept up with his schooling, but also taught him how to prepare meals and set the table. This would be the first time he'd used what he'd learned. Thankfully, his landlady, Mrs. Davis had nice china he could use to serve their dinner.

He took the last pieces of chicken out of the pan, set them on paper to drain then on a plate and covered them with a towel to keep in the heat. The green beans were done, as was the cornbread. It wasn't fancy, but hoped Leigh didn't mind. He checked the icebox and noted he had a near full pitcher of lemonade, then went about setting the table. Miles stepped back to survey his handiwork and smiled. Mama would be proud that he remembered where to place the napkins, silverware and glasses. A quick check of the time confirmed he had just enough time to take a bath.

Miles wanted to look his best and chose his new brown suit with a starched white shirt. Satisfied and, uncharacteristically nervous, he prayed the dinner went well and that he'd be able to keep his hands to himself. Though they'd been intimate, he needed her to see that what he felt went beyond physical desire.

CHAPTER 8

"This had to cost quite a sum," Liz said, surveying Leigh's sculpture.

Leigh ran a loving hand over the couple. "I know. I still can't believe he gave me such an expensive gift."

"And what a gift. I would love to know his motivation. This isn't some trivial object like a bowl. Look at them, the passion is clear as glass." Liz leaned back in her chair and folded her arms. "I told you Miles seems far more serious about you this time. I've seen several women propositioning him and he's turned them down flat. Even Belinda has been stomping mad because he won't pay her any attention."

Leigh didn't like hearing about all the women, though she couldn't blame them. With his height, good looks nice build and wonderful voice, he'd be a great catch for any woman. And she knew all about Belinda. The woman had been frosty toward Leigh for the past two weeks. But it did make her smile that Miles hadn't given any of them more than a passing glance. "He invited me for dinner this evening," she blurted.

Liz grinned. "Where's he taking you?"

She hesitated. "Um…he's cooking for me at his place."

"*Really?*" Liz sat up straight in her chair. "Can he cook?"

"I have no idea." The only thing he'd ever cooked for her was the bluegill fish he'd caught when they had gone on their picnic. Leigh had supplied the potato salad, biscuits and iced tea. "I don't even know what he's preparing. I figure he has to know something. He's been on his own since he was eighteen." She kept the rest of his story to herself. It still made her sad that he'd never had a permanent place to call home.

Liz lifted an eyebrow. "Exactly how old is Miles?"

"Twenty-eight. Only four years older than me."

"Better than Percy's fifteen," she said with a chuckle.

Leigh rolled her eyes. "Ugh. I'd take Miles over Percy even if he was *twenty* years older."

"I would, too. By the way, have you heard from your parents?"

She sighed. "No. I gave them my address and the telephone number to the restaurant. They don't have a telephone—or at least they didn't before I left—but a few of their church friends do. So does Mr. Butler's store." Most of the people back home who couldn't afford telephones had gone to the church or general store and were charged a few cents for each call. "I'd truly hoped they'd write. I guess they're still pretty upset." That she might never reconcile with her parents weighed heavily on Leigh's mind.

Liz patted Leigh's shoulder. "Maybe their letter is on the way. You know the post can be slow sometimes." She waved a hand. "Enough of that. What are you wearing to dinner?"

Leigh could always depend on her friend to make her smile. "I don't know."

She stood. "Well, let's go see what's in your closet."

After a good twenty minutes of going back and forth on her few dresses, Leigh couldn't decide. Every one she owned was laid out on the bed.

"I think you should wear this one." Liz held up a blue short-sleeved, V-neck dress with a drop waist.

"Okay." She hung up the other dresses.

"I'm going to leave so you can get ready. I have my own dinner date," Liz added with a sly smile.

"Well now. I'll make sure not to disturb you later." They both giggled like schoolgirls, shared a hug and Liz departed.

Afterward, Leigh pinned her hair up to keep it from getting wet and settled into a warm tub of water. She wanted to linger, but she and Liz had visited longer than expected and she still had to do her hair. She washed and dressed, then used her hair irons to curl her thick hair. She added some color on her lips, fastened the strand of pearls her parents had given her when she got her teaching certificate around her neck and sprayed a bit of her favorite perfume—a sweet floral scent with notes of vanilla. She heard the knock as she fastened her shoes. Taking a calming breath, she picked up her handbag and wrap and went to open the door.

"You look beautiful," Miles said before she could utter a greeting.

"And you look very handsome." The nice brown suit and white shirt looked new.

"Shall we?" He extended his arm.

Leigh locked the door and hooked her arm in his. Smiling, they made their way down the steps and to his car.

He helped her in, shut the door and went around to the driver's side. "I don't live that far away, but I didn't want you to have to walk."

"That's sweet, Miles. But I wouldn't have minded." She'd wondered how far away he lived and what type of place he had. He parked in front of a building only three blocks from The Magnolia. She turned her surprised gaze his way. "You're really close."

"I usually walk during the day, but I don't like to take chances being out on the streets like that at night too much."

She couldn't blame him with all the dangers. One of Liz's waiters had been robbed at knifepoint on his way home one night. He'd told Leigh, although he was upset about the money, it could be replaced. His life could not. Miles led her up to his apartment. He had a sofa and two chairs in the front room and a table with four chairs in the kitchen. There were no photos or other decorations that made a place a home, but it clean. "You don't have much here."

Miles laughed softly. "You said the same thing three years ago. I know what you're thinking and that's not the reason. I keep telling you I'm staying put. When I was growing up, we could only take what fit in one suitcase and I guess I never got out of the habit."

"I wasn't thinking that," she mumbled, trying to hide her smile.

"Uh huh."

"Whatever you cooked smells good," Leigh said to change the subject. She placed her wrap and handbag on a chair and followed him to the kitchen.

"It's nothing fancy."

She reached up to kiss his cheek. "I'm sure whatever you have will be just fine. And you set a lovely table."

An embarrassed expression crossed his face. "Thanks." Miles seated her then brought everything to the table. "Is lemonade okay?"

"Yes."

He poured some in her glass and his before taking the seat across from her. Taking her hand, he recited a short blessing. He gestured for her to fix her plate first.

Leigh placed the chicken, green beans with potatoes and cornbread on her plate, waited for him to fill his own before starting in on the meal. She ate silently for the first few minutes, more than a little impressed. The cornbread was light, the chicken seasoned to perfection and the green beans flavorful.

"Are you going to say something?" Miles asked, uncertainty in his voice.

"You've outdone yourself, Miles. This chicken tastes as good as mine. Where did you learn to cook like this?"

Relief washed over his face. "My grandmother."

"She taught you well." She went back to her food. "Do you have any pictures of your family?"

He looked up from his plate. "Just one of my folks on their wedding day." He dug it out of his pocket and handed it to her.

"Your mother was very beautiful and your father, handsome." Leigh could sense the love flowing from the couple in their smiles. "You look a lot like your father."

"That's what Mama says every time I visit her. That picture, my father's wedding ring and pocket watch are all I have of them."

She had wondered about the ring on his finger, but never got up the nerve to ask because she had been afraid of the answer. Though the wearing of a ring to show one's married status was popular for women, that didn't hold true for men. "At least you have something." She handed the picture back and they resumed eating. Seeing the photo brought the dilemma with her own parents to mind, but she pushed it aside. Miles had gone through a lot of trouble to make their dinner special and Leigh didn't want to ruin it.

As if sensing her thoughts, Miles asked, "Have your parents written back?"

Leigh shook her head.

He grasped her hand. "I'm sorry, Leigh."

She waved him off. "Don't worry about it. I'd rather talk about this outstanding meal. You wouldn't by chance want to make this a Sunday tradition?" She smiled sweetly. She'd eaten every bite on her plate.

Miles laughed so hard he had to leave the table to catch his breath. He came back, placed a kiss on her lips and said, "I'll cook for you every day of the week, and do any other thing you want, baby." He trailed kisses down her neck.

Her fork slipped unnoticed from her hand and hit the plate. Leigh closed her eyes and gave herself up to the wonderful sensations that his kisses always created. His hands mapped a path over her breasts and her breath hitched. He reclaimed her mouth, sliding his tongue provocatively around hers and causing her to lose all sense of time and place.

"Are you finished eating?"

"Yes," she whispered. He carried her over to the sofa and sat with her in his lap. The magnificent kisses began again and her dress was rucked up to her thighs. She slid her hand over his chest and along his jaw while he continued to tease her with tongue.

Miles eased back. "Woman, you make me lose myself. I promised myself I'd be on my best behavior."

"You're being *very* good." Leigh pulled his head back down for another spine-tingling kiss.

He groaned. "You're killing me, sweetheart. I want to do this courting thing right. I had planned to take you for ice cream before the sweet shop closed." He took out his pocket watch. "We have about thirty minutes if you want to go."

The only thing Leigh wanted was for him to take her to his bedroom and finish what he'd started. A scandalous thought, no doubt, but her body didn't care. However, she appreciated his efforts and knew it would be best for them to slow down. "I'd love some ice cream."

Miles righted her clothes and sat her on the sofa next to him. He closed his eyes and leaned his head back. "Give me a minute. You've got my body in an uproar."

"So is mine." She smoothed down her hair.

He rolled his head in her direction and eyed her.

"What? That's not something a woman is supposed to say?"

He just shook his head and chuckled. Rising to his feet, he helped her up. "Let's go. It's still light enough to walk if you want."

"I'd like that." They strolled to the shop hand-in-hand, enjoyed their dessert and walked back.

"I should probably take you home. If I don't, I'll break my promise."

"And we can't have that. You're a very special man, Miles."

"Would you like to take a plate home?"

"You'd better believe it," Leigh said with a laugh. "I never turn down fried chicken." They went back up for the food. He overrode her protest to help clean up and led her back to the car.

"Today was all for you. I want you to know how much I care for you. How much you mean to me."

The sweetness of his words poured over her and at that moment she fell completely in love with him. Again.

* * *

Miles and Leigh sat at a table sipping lemonade after the show on Tuesday night. "I have a surprise for you."

"You're going to cook for me again?" Leigh asked, her eyes brightening. "I enjoyed having my leftovers yesterday."

He smiled. "No. Something better."

"What is it?"

"I spoke to a man at Columbia Records about the song."

She jerked upright. Her heart started pounding. "And?"

"He said he wants to come hear us sing first before committing to anything." Miles had nearly burst at the seams with the news and couldn't wait to share it with Leigh.

She brought her hands to her mouth. "This might really happen," she whispered.

"I'm counting on it." He knew the moment Mr. Adams heard Leigh sing, the man would want to sign her exclusively. He opened his mouth to say something, but turned at the commotion near the front. "Looks like somebody doesn't want to leave."

"I'm sure Jacob and Oliver will handle it."

Miles had no doubt the two big bouncers could take care of the situation. Leigh gasped and he whipped his head around her way. She looked as if she'd seen a dead man.

"What is he doing here?" she whispered

He divided his gaze between Leigh and the man who broke away from Jacob's hold and rushed toward where he and Leigh were sitting.

"Well, well. If it isn't my runaway fiancée."

Fiancée? Miles's heart almost stopped. "Leigh?"

"I am not his fiancée," Leigh gritted out. "What are you doing here, Percy?"

"Your father sent me to bring you home."

"He *what*? You've come a long way for nothing because I will not be leaving." She turned to Miles. "I am not his fiancée no matter what he says."

Miles couldn't speak if his life depended on it. He shook his head to try to make sense of what was going on. Liz stood a short distance away with utter shock covering her face.

"So you're going to disobey your father? He sent a letter for me to give you." Percy smiled smugly and Leigh snatched the letter.

Leigh read silently and tossed it on the table. "It doesn't matter."

Miles picked it up and read: *Mary, do you know how worried your mother and I have been for the past three years? You should be ashamed of yourself. I want you to renounce that devil music and come home to marry Percy. He's been sick over missing you. We'll expect you within the week. Your Father.* He placed the note on the table. Anger surged through him with such force he had to clench his fists at his side to keep from flattening the pompous little jerk. Miles towered over the walrus looking man by a good five or six inches and he wanted to pound him into meal. He had to get out of here before he did something that would get him in trouble. He'd always had a temper and worked hard to keep it in check. But tonight, he was a second away from losing it. Without a word, he stalked toward the front, snatched the door open and slammed it behind him. Miles had wanted to explain to Leigh that he wasn't angry with her, but didn't trust himself to speak. He prayed she would listen to him once he cooled down.

* * *

Leigh watched Miles's departure and wanted to go after him. Things were finally going well with them and now her past had come calling.

"Guess you weren't as convincing to your little friend as you thought with the way he hightailed it out of here."

She turned her blazing gaze on Percy. "I'm not worried about him. I know he believes me." She pointed a finger in his face. "Listen to me, *Percival.* I can give you a letter carry back to my father if you like, but I will not be going. My life is here. Now get out!"

Jacob and Oliver took that as their cue and dragged Percy to the front and tossed him out the door.

Leigh dropped down wearily at the table and cradled her hands in her head. "Lord, why me?" Contrary to what she told Percy, she was worried about what Miles believed, especially since he'd read the note. The look on Miles's face had gone from shock and disbelief to anger in the blink of an eye. He'd most likely put the timeline when she left home together and because she had never mentioned Percy when she and Miles dated previously, in all probability, he didn't know what to believe. She felt a hand on her shoulder and lifted her head. "I guess you were right about that letter being on its way."

Liz lowered herself into the chair next to Leigh. "I don't know what to say."

"There's not much to say, except what I've already said." The night had started with so much promise—the man she loved had given her flowers before the show and had shared that the record deal might be a real possibility. Now it could all go away. The tears she had been trying to hold back flowed down her cheeks and she swiped at them. Liz handed her a handkerchief. "Thanks."

"Did Miles say anything before he left?"

Leigh shook her head. "I could see the hurt and anger in his eyes. I'm sorry, you're supposed to be closing." She started to stand.

"Sit." She turned to the two bouncers. "You can go home now. We'll be fine."

"You sure, Miss Liz?" Oliver asked. "What if he comes back?"

"All the lights are off except the small one here and I'll lock the door behind you."

"I don't know."

"We'll be going upstairs in a moment, I promise."

The two men stood there as if trying to decide whether to leave. Finally they agreed. "But we'll be back a little early tomorrow, just in case that idiot shows up."

"Thanks." Liz followed them to the door, locked it as promised and came back to the table. "Do you think Percy will come back?"

"I hope not. I don't need this right now." She'd told Percy everything he needed to know and had no intention of altering her stance. She was more concerned about Miles and what this meant for their relationship.

CHAPTER 9

Wednesday, Leigh put the dilemma with Percy and Miles aside and went to the dress shop. Although she didn't know where they stood personally, she knew Miles would let nothing come between their dreams of recording. He had mentioned the man from Columbia Records wanting to hear them first, but she had no idea when he might be coming. She wanted to look her very best and knew the perfect dress. She'd seen it a few weeks ago, but had to wait until she had enough to afford the twenty-four-dollar price tag.

"Well, hello, Leigh. Enjoyed that new song."

"Hello, Mrs. Boyd. I'm glad you enjoyed it," Leigh said to the shop owner. She nodded politely to the other two women standing nearby. They turned up their noses and went in the opposite direction. Obviously, they didn't approve of her occupation. She made her way to the section where she'd seen the dress previously and found it just where she remembered. The black and silver sequined dress had a low-cut neckline and thin straps that were designed to hang slightly off the shoulder. She carried it over to where Mrs. Boyd stood folding slips. "Mrs. Boyd, may I try this on?"

Mrs. Boyd placed the slip on the pile. "Of course." She led Leigh to the dressing room and helped her. "You're such a tiny thing. We'll need to alter this just a bit. Let me get my tapes and pins." She was gone and back in a flash.

Leigh stood still while the woman tugged and pinned and endured more than a few sticks. She wished she could just go into a store, pick out a ready-made dress and leave without all the fuss. Because of her petite stature, every time she shopped, this was the result.

"I can have it ready for you on Friday."

"That's fine." She carefully removed the dress and Mrs. Boyd exited. Leigh put on her clothes and went back out front. Her black T-strap shoes were worn and needed to be replaced. She tried on a few pairs and settled on one adorned with silver sequins on the straps. Next, she selected two pairs of stockings and carried everything to the counter. While waiting her turn in line, she spotted a necklace with black and silver beads that would complement the dress. Deciding that she deserved to splurge a bit, she added it to her purchases.

Mrs. Boyd rang everything up. "You can pay for the dress when you pick it up on Friday." She leaned closer and said conspiratorially, "I won't be charging you for the alterations."

Leigh smiled. "Thank you so much, Mrs. Boyd." Not many members of the race owned businesses and she made sure to patronize those who did.

"You can thank me by getting your music on one of those race records, so I can hear your pretty voice anytime I want. My husband bought me one of those fancy phonographs."

She laughed and took her bag. "I'll do my best. Have a nice day."

"You too, Leigh. See you Saturday night."

Leigh spent the balance of the afternoon reading portions of *The New Negro* by Alain Locke. She especially enjoyed the writings of Zora Neale Hurston and the poetry by Anne Spencer and Langston Hughes. After a dinner of collards, yams and ham, she dressed for the evening. She wanted to go down a little early to talk to Liz.

She took the stairs down and as she reached for the door and a hand yanked her back. Leigh spun and punched the offender in the face. He released his hold and staggered

Sheryl Lister

back. *Percy.* She turned to run and he caught her around the waist.

"You little *bitch!* Do you know how much trouble you've caused me?" Percy snarled.

"Take your hands off me!" She squirmed and fought, but couldn't get out of Percy's grip. "Problems with your little traveling singing group scheme?" His eyes widened for a split second. "Yes, I heard you talking at the church. And where is my sculpture you stole?"

An evil grin crossed his lips. "It fetched a good price." His featured hardened. "You caused me quite a bit of problems by leaving, but that's all over. Now quit moving. You're coming with me."

Leigh renewed her struggle. "No! Let me go."

The door opened and Miles was across the space in a flash. He slammed Percy against the wall and held him there with his forearm across Percy's throat. "You okay, Leigh?"

"Yes," she answered, still shaken. Percy clawed at Miles's arm, trying to breathe.

Not taking his eyes off Percy, Miles said, "Go on inside, baby. Percy and I need to have a little chat."

"Miles—"

"Don't worry, I only plan to talk. Go on now. I'll join you in a minute."

Percy looked her way pleadingly. Surely he didn't expect her to intervene. "Okay. Enjoy your chat, Percy." As much she wanted to get rid of Percy, she didn't want Miles to do anything to jeopardize his freedom.

* * *

"So, you like manhandling women?" Miles pressed his arm a little tighter against Percy's throat.

"Let me go, or I'm going to the police," Percy choked out.

100

"Is that before or after you tell them you assaulted a woman in a hallway? Let me give you a piece of advice. Don't ever let me catch you with your hands on Leigh again. Get on the train and go back to wherever you came from and you'll live a long life."

Still struggling and clawing, he rasped out, "You can't threaten me."

Miles smiled coldly. "Nah, it's not a threat." Percy opened his mouth to say something and Miles stuck his colt right between Percy's eyes. "It's a promise. Get my meaning?"

Percy's eyes went wide and he nodded vigorously.

He released his hold and Percy slumped to the floor, coughing and gasping for air. Miles slid the colt back into its holster and hauled Percy up by his collar. "And just so you know, I don't like to repeat myself." He dragged him to the door, opened it and caught Oliver's eye. The big man rushed over. "Can you put the trash out?"

"With pleasure," Oliver said.

Miles left Oliver to handle Percy and sought out Leigh. His plan had been to arrive early and talk to her about what happened last night. He hadn't expected to find her being shoved around by Percy and was glad he'd gotten there when he did. He came up behind her at the bar. "Hey, baby."

Leigh whirled on the stool and threw her arms around him. "Miles. I was so worried." She looked him over critically and palmed his face.

"I'm fine."

"Where's Percy?"

"Oliver is taking care of him."

"You didn't—"

Miles chuckled. "No, I didn't kill him." He turned serious. "I warned him to stay away from you is all. I hope he takes me at my word."

"I'm so sorry about all of this. Can we go to the dressing room to talk?"

"Sure." He led her out of the club and held the door open for her to enter. Leigh sat in one of the upholstered armchairs and he lowered himself into the one next to her. "I came early to talk to you about last night." He got mad all over again thinking about Percy with his hands on her. "I'm glad I got here when I did."

"So am I." Leigh wrung her hands. "I know you're upset and I can't blame you, but I'm not his fiancée."

He leaned forward, took her hands in his and brought them to his lips. "Sweetheart, I'm not angry with you and I believe you."

"But last night you left and I thought…"

"Leigh, I did leave last night because I was angry, not at you, but Percy. I wanted to strangle him on sight and in order to keep myself from doing that, I left."

Relief flooded her face and water filled her eyes. "You don't know how glad I am to hear you say that."

Miles wiped away the tear running down her soft brown cheek. "You're not getting rid of me that easily. But I need you to tell me about Percy."

Leigh gave him a watery smile. "I should have told you before. He's the pastor's nephew and was visiting from somewhere. I never asked because I didn't care. He was supposed to be there for two weeks, but apparently decided to stay in Magnolia. Anyway, he heard me singing in the choir one Sunday morning and after that, he followed me around every week asking if he could call on me. I kept saying no, but he wasn't deterred. Somehow, he struck it up with my father. Percy gave him some sad story about starting a church, said he was looking for a wife and asked my father's permission to court me. I told my father I wasn't interested."

He angled his head, confused. "Then how did the whole engagement come about?"

"My father knew I wanted to leave Magnolia to become a jazz singer. He said marrying Percy would settle me down properly." She shook her head. "I told my father that I overheard Percy talking about wanting to start a traveling singing group, that he was lying about starting a church, but he didn't believe me."

Miles couldn't believe her father would take the word of a man he'd recently met over that of his daughter. But times being as they were, women were still expected to defer to a man. "I'm sorry."

"Percy got himself invited to dinner a couple of times, showed up unannounced and I was forced to sit with him in the front room." Fire leaped into her eyes. "On one of those visits, he asked about a sculpture sitting on the mantle. I used a good portion of the money I'd been saving for New York to purchase it and he stole it."

His anger flared again. "Did you get it back?"

"No. I asked him about it earlier and he said he'd sold it."

"Be glad I didn't know that then. I'd have gotten every penny back if I'd had to take it out of his hide."

She grabbed Miles hands. "Please don't do anything crazy. I don't want you to get into any trouble."

"That depends on Percy. I told him to get back on the train and warned him what would happen if he came near you again. But I don't trust that he'll do that." Miles cut off her protest with a kiss. "Don't fight me on this, sweetheart.

Any man who would travel this far for a woman he knows doesn't want him isn't playing with a full deck. Is he still talking about this scheme?"

Leigh nodded. "He said something about my leaving causing him problems, but that it would be over now if he took me back."

"I don't like the sound of that. I don't want you going anywhere alone."

"Miles, I can't just stop my errands. I need to go to the market tomorrow, pick up my dress from Mrs. Boyd's shop on Friday and do a host of other things."

"Then go with Liz or somebody else. Better yet, I'll go with you." The more he thought about it, the more he was convinced that would be the best choice. Percy wouldn't dare try anything with him around. "I'm not going to let him anywhere near you." A knock interrupted his next words. "I'll get it."

"Fifteen minutes," the announcer said when Miles opened the door.

"Thanks. I'll be right out." Miles closed the door and hunkered down in front of Leigh. "I don't know what I'd do if something happened to you." Miles bowed his head briefly. Just the thought made his chest tighten with fear. "I couldn't take it. So let me take care of you, protect you like I should have three years ago."

"I don't want anything to happen to you, either."

He covered her mouth in a heated kiss. "See you in a minute." Miles went out and before taking his place at the piano, asked the two bouncers to keep an eye out for Percy. Watching Leigh perform, one would never know the turmoil going on, but he knew and vowed to do everything in his power to keep her safe.

After the show, instead of hanging around until closing Miles escorted Leigh up to her place. He didn't want to leave her alone and considered camping out until they knew for sure that Percy left town.

Leigh removed her shoes and came to where he still stood near the door. She wrapped her arms around his waist. "Is something bothering you?"

"I don't want you to be here alone."

She looked up at him. "Percy can't get in the building without a key and the club is locked at night. Oliver and Jacob said they would keep an eye on the side door to make sure he doesn't sneak back there again. I'll be fine." She led him over to the sofa. "Come sit with me for a while. Do you want something to drink?"

Miles removed his suit coat and hat and placed them on the chair. "No, thanks. I just want to hold you." Miles scooter closer until their bodies were touching and draped an arm around her shoulder. He kissed the top of her head and she placed her head on his chest. His emotions swelled. He wanted to see her face each night before he closed his eyes and when he opened them every sunrise, sit on the porch of their home talking and holding hands, make her every dream come true and spend the rest of his life loving her. Miles tilted her chin and captured her mouth in a slow kiss, feeding on the sweetness inside. Leigh held him in place and he had no problem with that. He could kiss her all night, but other parts of his body had other ideas. She boldly ran a hand over his erection and he grew harder with each stroke. On the brink of release, he stilled her hand.

"Problems?" she asked with a sultry smile.

Miles surged to his feet, lifted her in his arms and carried her to bed. "Nope. None at all. Problems?"

"Just one."

"What's that?"

"You're going too slow."

Miles threw his head back and roared with laughter. "Then let's see if I can speed things up." He had her naked in the blink of an eye. He caressed her breasts then circled his tongue around one sable-tipped nipple then the other, while his hand continued to blaze a trail over her stomach, hips, thighs and back up to her wet center. Her hips rose to his play and her breathless moans stoked the fire building in his body.

"Miles, I...*ohh*." She arched and came, calling his name.

He watched her ride out her passions then stood and removed his clothes. He sheathed himself in the rubber, climbed on the bed and kissed his way up her body. Miles parted her legs and eased himself inside. He shuddered, feeling her so tight around him. She ran her hands over his chest and, as always, her touch elicited a multitude of emotions that he had been unable to define. Until now. He started moving, slowly at first and gradually increased the pace. Without missing a beat, he rolled over onto his back, pulling her on top of him. She met each of his upward strokes with one of her own. Miles leaned up and took one erect nipple into his mouth. He suckled it then the other, all while keeping the same pace. Their blended cries mingled in the room, playing the melody of his heart. Her body trembled and her muscles clenched him as release washed over her again. Gripping her hips, he thrust faster and deeper. His orgasm sped through him in a searing burst of passion that forced a low groan from his throat.

Leigh collapsed on top of him and let out a sigh of pleasure. "You're really good at this."

"So are you." Miles idly ran his hand up and down her spine. "I love you, Leigh."

Her head popped up. "What did you say?"

"I love you."

She stared at him for a long moment. "Truly?"

"Truly."

"I love you, too."

Miles smiled and pulled her down for a kiss that left them both panting. He held her close, not wanting to leave, but knowing he had no choice.

"I wish you didn't have to leave."

"Me, too." He lay there a few minutes more before getting up and putting on his clothes. "What time do you need to shop tomorrow?"

"I usually go around ten."

"I'll be here shortly before then. Good night."

"Good night and be careful."

"I will."

Miles got in his car and before he could drive one block, he saw the police behind him. He pulled over and waited. One came to the driver's side and the other went around to the passenger side. He kept both hands on the steering wheel and didn't move, not wanting to give them any reason to shoot him. Not that they'd need one.

The policeman on his side glanced inside the car. "You out kind of late, boy."

The slur tightened Miles's jaw, but he said nothing.

"Where are you coming from?"

"I play piano over at The Magnolia Club, sir."

His eyes swept over the interior again. "Didn't they shut down over an hour ago?"

"Yes, sir. But I was visiting with my lady friend, who lives in the apartments above." Beads of perspiration dotted his forehead and his hands shook.

He stood there, as if looking for some other reason that Miles had been out. "You have papers for this car?"

"Yes, sir. In my inner pocket. May I?" At the man's nod, Miles slowly extracted the folded paper and handed it to him. He held it up to catch the light of the lamppost and stared at it so long, Miles worried he wouldn't give it back.

Finally, he handed it back. "Where you headed?"

"Just two streets over to my place, sir."

"Well, get on over there then."

"Yes, sir." Miles waited until the policemen got back into their car before starting his and continuing on to his apartment. They followed. He parked, unlocked the outer door and went inside. They drove on. Miles released the breath he didn't realize he'd been holding.

The incident had soured his good mood, but as he lay in bed later, thoughts of Leigh's confession that she loved him lifted his spirits. He'd do whatever it took to keep her safe because he wanted her as his wife.

CHAPTER 10

"Good morning, beautiful. Ready to go pick up that dress?" Miles stood leaning against the door wearing a dark blue suit, giving Leigh that heart-melting smile.

Initially, Leigh wasn't too keen on having Miles escort her everywhere, but found she enjoyed his company immensely. He'd paid for her purchases at the market yesterday and she, in turn, cooked dinner for him. "I am." She picked up her handbag from the nearby table, took his extended arm and he escorted her out. "Any idea when the man from the record company plans to come hear us sing?"

"I actually wanted to talk to you about that. He asked if I could meet him this afternoon at two. I spoke with Liz before coming up to get you and she said it would be okay for us to meet in the restaurant. I'd like you to be there, too."

"I'd love to come, but are you sure he'll be okay with it. Some men don't like to deal with women directly."

"He'll deal with both of us, so it should be fine."

"Well, when you put it that way," she said with a laugh. "Count me in." He opened the door for her to enter Mrs. Boyd's shop. Every woman stopped and turned their way. Leigh walked over to the counter to wait her turn and Miles stayed over by the door. She noticed the smiles on all the women's faces.

"You sure can play that piano, Mr. Cooper," one woman said.

Miles tipped his hat politely. "Thank you, ma'am."

The woman giggled like an adolescent and Leigh rolled her eyes.

"Hi, Leigh. Your dress is all ready. Come on back and try it on."

"Thank you, Mrs. Boyd." She tried it on, pleased that no other alterations would be needed.

"You look lovely, dear."

She certainly felt that way. "I love it."

When they came back, Mrs. Boyd seemed to notice Miles for the first time.

"Oh, my word. That's Miles Cooper. Can't wait to hear you play on Saturday," Mrs. Boyd called out with a wave.

Miles smiled.

"Lord, that smile will make a woman willingly cross the line into sin."

Leigh chuckled. That was the truth.

"Not that I'm complaining, but men don't usually come into a women's shop."

She couldn't tell the real reason Miles had come. "He graciously offered to accompany me before we meet discuss some music." She counted out what she owed and collected her dress. "See you soon."

When she reached the door, Miles asked, "Do you want me to carry it?"

"No, but thank you." They started back up the street. She'd wanted to ask about making a few modifications to the song, but didn't want to offend Miles. She decided to ask anyway. "Miles, do you think I can change a few lines of the song?"

"Of course. Baby, that's *our* song. You can change anything you want. We have some time before meeting Mr. Adams. We can do it at your place or mine."

"Mine. That way if we lose track of time, we only need to go downstairs." The last time they'd written a song together, six hours had passed before either of them realized it. "Do you think Percy left town?"

"If he had any sense, he did."

If he had any sense, he wouldn't have come in the first place in Leigh's mind. She hadn't seen him and Liz confirmed that he didn't come to the club last night. "Let's hope so." She planned to write her parents again and tell them about the incident in the hallway. Surely her father wouldn't condone such behavior. Back in her apartment, Leigh hung up her dress. She found Miles seated at the kitchen table with the music in front of him. "You want something to drink?"

"No, thanks." Miles lit a cigarette.

She placed an ashtray in front of him and sat.

He pushed the sheets and a pen her way. "What were you thinking about changing?"

Leigh studied the lyrics. They went back and forth for a time discussing some of the modifications. "And then some phrases on the lines I'll sing, like right here." She pointed. "I want to say, with each touch you set my soul on fire, and I love when you kiss me in that special way I desire." She glanced up to see Miles staring at her strangely. "What?"

Miles exhaled smoke and set the cigarette on the ashtray. "Is that what you feel when I touch and kiss you?"

"Yes," she said, softer than intended.

He covered her hand with his. "And every day when the sun rises, your voice is the first thing on my mind. It's the music of my heart, a rare and precious find."

Part of the lyrics he'd sang to her that day, the words moved her even more today. She felt herself being drawn into his sensual spell. He stroked the back of her hand, brought it to his lips and placed a lingering kiss there. Leigh's pulse skipped.

"That's what I feel about you, Leigh. You *are* a rare and precious find, and I'm glad you're mine."

Sheryl Lister

Leigh melted against the chair. "Miles—"

"I know, sweetheart. We'll save it for later." He sat back. "Anything else you want to change?"

"Just one more thing." Instead of speaking the words out loud, she wrote them on the paper. He read what she wrote and desire flared in his eyes.

"So, my loving takes your breath away? I've a confession. Yours takes mine away, too."

Oh, mercy! "Um…did you decide on a title?"

"Love's Serenade."

That summed it up perfectly. Leigh pushed away from the table. "I think it's time to go. We don't want to be late."

Miles chuckled knowingly and stood. "No, we don't."

"I want to freshen up a bit. Can I meet you downstairs?"

"Sure thing."

She waited until he closed the door and scrubbed a hand across her forehead. "That man makes me lose myself."

When she went downstairs, she spotted Miles at a table on the far side of the restaurant. "Hello, Belinda."

Belinda eyed her. "Leigh. I assume you want a table."

"I'll be joining Miles."

"Is that so? He told me he's waiting for a Mr. Adams. It's a little rude of you to interrupt, but I'm sure that's nothing new."

Leigh raised an eyebrow. The woman had been dancing on Leigh's last nerve ever since she found out she and Miles were seeing each other. "Not if I've been invited." She spun on her heel and strode over to the table. She heard Belinda mutter something, but she didn't care. Miles stood at Leigh's approach and seated her. "Thanks. Did you order yet?"

"No. I thought I'd wait until Mr. Adams arrives."

They didn't have to wait long.

Belinda escorted him over and placed a menu on the table. "Welcome to The Magnolia. I'll be back in a moment to take your order."

Mr. Adams removed his hat and nodded. He turned to Miles and extended his hand. "Mr. Cooper, nice to see you again."

Miles rose and shook his hand. "Same here. I'd like you to meet Miss Leigh Jones."

Mr. Adams smiled. "It's nice to finally meet you, Miss Jones." He took the chair opposite Leigh.

"It's nice to meet you, as well, Mr. Adams." He was of average height, had dark skin and a razor-thin mustache that added an air of danger to his handsome face.

"I have to admit, I've been looking forward to hearing you sing. I caught the last few bars of your performance over at the Winston's rent party a few months ago. I'd hoped to be able to hear more."

"That's very kind of you to say," she said.

Belinda came and took Mr. Adams's and Miles's order. "Oh, Leigh, you don't have a menu?"

Leigh wanted to smack her. She had purposely not given Leigh a menu. "Don't worry about it, Belinda. I already know what I want," she said sweetly. "I'll have the fried filet of sole, tartar sauce and potatoes, and tea."

Belinda shot Leigh a hostile glare and walked off.

"So, Miles, you mentioned a song. How long will it take for it to be ready?"

Miles shared a look with Leigh. "Is tomorrow good? Music starts here at nine."

A wide grin covered Mr. Adams's face. "I'll be here. If it's as good as you say, we'll see about getting you two in the studio. We want to strike while the iron is hot, and right now the race records are selling well."

Leigh tried to contain her excitement. She glanced at Miles and he winked.

"Sounds good." Miles faced Leigh. "Is that okay with you, Miss Jones?"

"Yes." And she knew just what dress to wear.

* * *

Miles couldn't believe he was finally close to realizing his dream. Since Liz only opened on Saturdays for dinner, he and Leigh had plenty of time to practice and still allow her to rest her voice. He dug out his pocket watch. He was due to meet Leigh at one, but wanted to get there a few minutes early. He started toward his bedroom, but stopped upon hearing a knock. Miles reversed his course, opened the door and all hell broke loose. Two men grabbed him and shoved him inside. Because Miles was taller than both, he used it to his advantage. He elbowed the one closest to him and when he staggered back, Miles punched his partner, who was out cold before he hit the floor. The first man rushed Miles and they fell onto the sofa. The blow momentarily knocked the wind out of Miles, but he came up swinging and when the dust settled, his opponent lay writhing on the floor. Breathing heavily, Miles stalked over and grabbed his colt from the drawer. He dragged the man up and tossed him none to gently into the chair. There was only one person who could be responsible. "Did Percy send you?"

"Go to hell," the man spat.

Miles calmly shot him in the knee. "The next one's going to send you to reserve my seat."

"*Ow!* You shot me," he screamed, grabbing his knee and sliding to the floor.

His partner stirred and sat up wide-eyed. The gun in Miles's hand must have scared him because he started scooting away. "My temper's not real good right now, so you've got one chance to answer my question. Where did Percy take Leigh?" When he didn't answer fast enough, Miles strode over, snatched him up and stuck the gun in his face.

The man's eyes widened. "The train station, the train station," he squealed. "Please don't shoot me again."

"What time is the train scheduled to leave?"

"Two o'clock."

Miles tossed the still whimpering man aside. "Be gone when I get back or I'm going to send you and your friend to the undertaker." He snatched the door open. "And don't bleed all over Mrs. Davis's nice furniture and floor."

He took off down the stairs, jumped into his car and roared off. Mindful of what happened the other night and not wanting to have another run-in with the police, he eased off the pedal. The train wouldn't leave for another forty-five minutes, so he had plenty of time to get there. He'd promised Leigh he wouldn't do anything to get in trouble, but all bets were off.

Miles barely stopped the car before he was out and striding to the front of the train station. Pulling his hat down to partially hide his face, he snaked his way through the crowd of people milling about, took up a spot against the side of the building and scanned the area. The whistle blew, signaling the train's arrival. More than likely, Percy would try to board as quickly as possible. Miles peered through the window, but didn't see them. His apprehension went up a notch. What if they'd left on an earlier train? He left his position to check the schedule and went still. *Leigh.* Relief flooded him. He scrutinized her face to see if she'd been hurt, but couldn't tell from this distance.

115

Miles ducked inside the depot, exited through the opposite door and eased close to them. The glint of Percy's knife caught his attention and it took all he had to stick with his plan.

"Miles is going to hunt you down like the rabid dog you are, Percy," he heard Leigh say, still moving closer.

Percy laughed. "If you're waiting for pretty boy to rescue you, you'll be waiting a long time. He's going to be busy for quite a while."

Miles pressed his colt in Percy's back. "Actually, my schedule just opened up."

"Miles." Tears filled Leigh's eyes.

"You okay, Leigh?"

"Yes."

"Leigh, step away and Percy, hand me that knife real slow. I don't want to have to shoot you right here." Grumbling, Percy did as asked. "Let's go."

Leigh placed a hand on Mile's arm. "Where are you taking him?"

"To talk." He nudged Percy and marched him behind the station. "What part of our last conversation did you not understand, the part about me not liking to repeat myself or you getting out of town for your good health?"

Percy puffed up. "You're not going to shoot me?"

He smiled coldly. "You sure about that? I don't think your friend will agree with you."

"Wha…what are you talking about?"

"I thought that would get your attention. The only thing keeping me from leaving your carcass to rot, is my promise to Leigh." He holstered the gun and, without warning, crashed his fist into Percy's face. He followed the man down, landing blow after blow.

"Miles!"

Miles felt someone pulling him and finally Leigh's voice filtered through his rage.

"Miles, please stop. *Please.*"

He hoisted Percy to his feet and searched his pockets. He found the train tickets. "Hold these," he said to Leigh. Miles continued his search and relieved Percy of every penny in his pockets.

"Hey! You can't take my money," Percy wailed.

"This is payment for stealing Leigh's sculpture." He half dragged, half walked Percy to the front. "You have a train to catch." He took the tickets from Leigh, gave her the money and escorted Percy to where the passengers were boarding. The conductor eyed Percy critically. Miles said nothing and handed him the ticket. He leaned close to Percy's ear. "If you ever step foot in Harlem again, I will shoot you on sight."

Percy turned his malevolent glare on Leigh.

Leigh smiled "Have a nice trip, Percy."

Miles chuckled and hauled Leigh into his arms. "Are you sure you're okay? I was so worried." He lightly ran his hands up and down her arm and searched her for any bruises or scrapes. "Did he hurt you?" He was so relieved to have her in his arms again

"No, no. Thank you for getting here when you did."

He brushed his lips across hers. "Let's go home, baby."

"Gladly." They headed toward the car. "Do you think we can stop at the telegraph office first?"

"Okay." He drove the short distance to the office. "Who are you sending a wire to?"

"My parents. I want them to know about Percy's lies and him trying to kidnap me at knifepoint," she said angrily.

117

When Leigh wrote what she wanted to send, the telegraph officer read it. "You sure you want to send this?"

"Yes. If there's a reply, you can send it here." Leigh scribbled her address on a piece of paper. That done, she and Miles returned to the car. She blew out a long breath. "At least that's over."

Miles reached for her hand. "You've been through a lot today. Do you want me to get word to Mr. Adams to postpone his visit tonight?"

"No. I'm fine. I hope we can still squeeze in a little time to rehearse before Liz opens up."

Miles could care less about a recording contract right now, he wanted to wrap Leigh in his arms and never let go. "Baby, maybe you should just rest tonight. I'm sure the audience will be fine for one night."

Leigh placed her hand against his cheek. "Miles, you are such an amazing man and I know you're concerned. I really am fine. How can I not be when I have you as my knight in shining armor?"

He slanted her a glance. "I love you."

"I love you, too." She rubbed her hands together with glee. "Let's give Mr. Adams a show he'll never forget."

"Whatever my baby wants." Miles smiled. This settling down thing might not be so bad after all.

CHAPTER 11

Leigh could hardly contain her excitement. Eight hours ago, she believed she'd be on her way back to a life of misery, but thanks to Miles she never had to worry about Percy again. He'd told her about the two men Percy sent. She shuddered at the thought of them hurting Miles. Although she wasn't a fan of him carrying a gun, today she'd been grateful to have it protecting her. In fact, if she'd had one she would have shot Percy herself. Percy had deserved that beating. Her anger rose again. She wondered if her parents would respond or if they would lay the blame at her doorstep. Leigh shook her head and pushed her speculations aside. Tonight, she would only concentrate on singing her best.

She and Miles agreed to keep the song a surprise until the end. Leigh hadn't even shared the information with Liz for fear of getting her hopes up for nothing. She decided to wait until they actually signed the contract. She heard the music, took a deep breath and surveyed her look in the mirror. The dress flowed seamlessly over her curves and the necklace complimented it perfectly. "Show time."

On stage, she and Miles shared a secret smile. He looked quite handsome in his black pants, white shirt, bow tie, suspenders and black fedora. When it came time for their new duet, butterflies started dancing in her stomach. Miles rose from the piano and walked the few steps to the center of the stage, as he did at the end of every show and the audience applauded.

Miles held up his hand and waited for them to quiet. "Miss Leigh and I have a special treat that we hope you'll enjoy. It's called Love's Serenade." He gave her hand a gentle squeeze of reassurance.

Sam, Willie and Loyce stared on in confused. Leigh saw Miles speak to them for a brief moment. The men smiled and nodded. Miles slid onto the piano bench. The moment the music started, every emotion she felt for Miles bubbled to the surface and with every word she sang, she tried to communicate exactly that to him. They'd sung many songs together, but only this one told of their own love story. Liz always kept a vase of flowers on the piano. Tonight after the song ended, Miles withdrew one of the white roses, presented it to her and placed a soft kiss on the back of her hand. Leigh looked out over the room. Some of the women had handkerchiefs out, dabbing at the corners of their eyes. Miles helped her down the steps and Leigh went over to the bar.

Without asking, Liz placed a glass of water in front of Leigh. "You and I need to talk. I can't believe you're keeping secrets," she groused.

She laughed. "Yes, we do." As she brought the glass to her lips, she saw Miles talking to Mr. Adams. Both men smiled and shook hands. Mr. Adams tipped his hat Leigh's way and exited.

"Who is that man and what was that all about?"

Leigh just smiled and sipped.

"Some friend you are."

"I'll tell you as soon as I can. I promise." She wanted to blurt out everything, but held back. First she needed to talk to Miles. She hoped those smiles meant something good. In the crowd of people, it took him almost ten minutes to make it over to the bar. Leigh was fairly bursting at the seams, and it took all her control not to pounce on him the moment he sat next to her. She waited for him to say something and, after a couple of minutes, prompted, "Well?"

"Monday morning at nine, contracts and then he'll schedule us for the studio."

Leigh launched herself at him and squealed with delight.

Laughing, Miles said, "You're giving folks a lot to talk about."

She didn't care. "Oh, my goodness! I can't believe it." She brought her hands to her mouth. Her dream was close to becoming reality.

"Believe it, sweetheart."

"I don't know how to thank you, Miles." Had he not come back into her life, she might have never had this opportunity.

"I didn't do anything. You did all the work. The world deserves to hear your beautiful voice." Miles stood. "May I walk you home?"

"I'd love for you to walk me home." Typically, Leigh had always been careful to keep their interactions businesslike in public. This time she wanted to shout to world how much she loved him.

* * *

Monday morning, Leigh sat nervously listening to Mr. Adams going over the contract details. She had no idea about what was acceptable, but Miles appeared to be very knowledgeable on the subject. Where she would have been satisfied with the promised pay to make the record, he demanded and got Mr. Adams to agree to also compensate them for songwriting and a portion for every record sold.

"Now, Mr. Adams, we're not going to have to worry about hearing our song on another record label under a false name, right?"

She turned her stunned gaze to Miles. She'd heard about singers and musicians being cheated, especially members of the race. Did record companies really do that?

"Of course not," Mr. Adams said. Though he seemed a bit uncomfortable.

Miles leaned back and folded his arms. "Good to know. Just didn't want to worry about what happened over at Gennett Records happening here."

"You have my word, Mr. Cooper."

He nodded and shifted his gaze to Leigh. "Anything you want to add, Leigh?"

"No. I think you covered everything." That he wanted to make sure they weren't taken advantage of made her love him even more. They read over each page and, with all the questions answered and issues settled, Leigh affixed her name in the indicated places, as did Miles. The bank draft he handed each of them widened Leigh's eyes.

Mr. Adams collected the papers, sorted them, then handed a copy to Leigh and Miles. "I know I said we'd schedule the studio recording for next week, but I'm hoping you have time to do it now."

"Now?" Leigh hadn't considered she be singing today.

"Unless you have a more pressing engagement."

"I'm free if Miles is."

Miles grinned. "Let's go make some music, baby."

Leigh's heart beat double time with excitement as she stepped into the studio. The small room had chairs, a piano and a series of microphones on long stands. It took three hours to get the perfect recording. Her back and feet hurt and she was starving, but the result would be worth every ache.

"I think we should celebrate tonight," Miles said as they drove to her apartment.

"You do remember we still have to work tonight."

He wiggled his eyebrows. "*After.*"

Heat stung her cheeks and she averted her gaze, but she couldn't stop the smile spreading across her lips.

"No? Yes?"

"Yes." Leigh's stomach rumbled. "But right now I'm starving. Do you want to come up for lunch?"

"I'd better not. Otherwise, I might be the only one eating."

It took her a moment to understand his meaning. She gasped softly. "Miles Cooper."

His laughter filled the car's interior. He dropped her off in front of the restaurant. "I'll see you tonight."

Leigh scooted over and placed a kiss on his clean-shaven cheek. "Okay." Instead of going up to her apartment, she went in search of Liz and found her poring over some papers in the small back room she used as an office. She knocked on the partially open door.

Liz's head came up. "Well, if it isn't my traitorous best friend. Come on in."

She entered with a smile and closed the door. "I want to tell you something."

"Is this about that secret?"

"Yes." Leigh withdrew the papers from her handbag and passed them to her friend. Liz read for a moment and her eyes lit up.

"Oh, my word. Does this mean what I think it does?"

"*Yes!*"

Liz was up and around the desk in the blink of an eye. She grabbed Leigh up in a sisterly embrace. "Oh, oh. This is so wonderful." She cried, Leigh cried, and then they laughed. Still wiping her eyes, she said, "This is exactly what you needed after that mess with Percy." Leigh had shared the details of what happened at the train station. "I am so proud of you."

"I would've never had this chance if it wasn't for you. I owe you."

"I just did what any friend would do."

"And I appreciate it more than you'll ever know." Her stomach growled again. "I need to find some food. As soon as the record is pressed, you'll get the first copy, after mine, of course," Leigh added with a laugh.

Liz joined her laughter. "Of course."

They shared another hug and Leigh floated up to her place. She'd never been so happy in her life. Automatically, her thoughts shifted to Miles and his proposed celebration. Her body throbbed in anticipation.

While eating, she leafed through her mail. She still hadn't heard from her parents. One envelope with a foreign stamp caught her attention. She quickly tore it open and read. She'd been invited to sing a jazz festival in Paris. Leigh reread the letter again to be sure the words were correct. She jumped up and did a dance. Her excitement was tempered by the fact that she'd be gone from The Magnolia for almost a month. And away from Miles. She couldn't ask him to accompany her and leave Liz without anyone. It would be bad enough that she'd need to find a singer, but if she had to replace Miles, it might affect business. Leigh couldn't, wouldn't let that happen.

* * *

Miles hadn't stopped smiling since he left the studio, and knowing that he'd have Leigh to himself in less than half an hour, had him chomping at the bit to finish the set. The moment it ended, he wasted no time hurrying them upstairs. Once there, he could only stare at the alluring picture she made seated on the sofa with her head thrown back and eyes closed. His gaze made a slow tour up her smooth brown legs and the curve of her breasts pressed against her dress to the luscious painted lips that never stopped calling to him. He crossed the room and lowered himself next to her. She opened her eyes and smiled, sending a jolt to his chest. "You take my breath away, Miss Leigh Jones." He traced a finger over her lips then placed a soft kiss on them. He treated her to a series of heated kisses along the scented column of her neck, bare shoulders and valley between her breasts. "Are you ready to celebrate?"

"I'm ready for you to take my breath away with your lovin'."

That's all Miles needed to hear. He scooped her up and carried her to the bedroom. He planned for them to celebrate all night and wake up in the morning and do it all again. As he stared down at her, one thing was clear. He wanted her as his wife, sooner rather than later.

The next morning, after another round of lovemaking, he propped on his elbow and watched Leigh sleep. His heart swelled with the magnitude of his love for her. She looked so peaceful he hated to wake her. But he wanted to let her know he was leaving. He kissed her awake.

"Hey," Leigh said sleepily.

"I just wanted to let you know I'm leaving. I'll see you this evening."

"There's something I need to talk to you about."

"We'll talk tonight."

"Mmm hmm." She closed her eyes again.

Miles gave her a gentle kiss, dressed and locked the door behind him. When he got home, he bathed and slept for the next four hours. He woke up feeling refreshed and padded to the kitchen to make a sandwich. Two bites in, someone knocked on his door. He groaned and went to answer it. "Hi, Mrs. Davis," he said to the older woman.

"Hi, Miles. Sorry to disturb you, but this was just delivered. I thought it might be important."

He took the telegram from her hand. "Thank you. Let me repay you for the delivery tip." He handed her a dollar.

"Son, I didn't tip this much."

"I know, but take it anyway."

Mrs. Davis smiled. "I wish I had a son like you. I'll let you get on with your day."

"Thanks, again." He tore open the envelope and the message almost dropped him to his knees. "No," he whispered. "Not Mama." One of his uncles had wired to let him know that his grandmother was ill and they wanted him to come as soon as possible.

Miles wolfed down the remainder of his sandwich. Used to packing at a moment's notice, it didn't take long to gather up his things. He stopped to explain his situation to Mrs. Davis and paid her two weeks advance rent. "If I'll be gone longer, I'll let you know."

"Don't worry about your place. I'll hold it as long as you need. You just go on and see about your grandmother. I'll add her to the prayer list at my church."

"I appreciate that." He rushed out, tossed the suitcase and satchel in the back seat and drove over to The Magnolia. His knock on Leigh's door went unanswered, so he checked the restaurant. "Belinda, have you seen Leigh?"

"No. Not since she and Elizabeth left an hour ago."

He ran an agitated hand down his face. He wanted to wait for her, but he needed to get to Louisiana. He grabbed a piece of paper and a pen off the hostess stand and scribbled a note telling Leigh that he had to see about his grandmother and that he'd be back in a week or so, if everything went well.

He also asked her to apologize to Liz. He folded it and gave it to Belinda. "Can you give this to Leigh when she comes back?"

"Sure." Belinda followed him to the door and stood watching as he jumped into his car and drove off. If he hurried, he could stop at the telegraph office to wire his uncle about his arrival time and make the three thirty train. Miles settled into the seat just as the whistle blew. He should be in Louisiana by this time tomorrow. He bowed his head and did something he hadn't done in a long time. Prayed.

When he stepped off the train the following afternoon, his clothes were wrinkled and travel worn and so was his body from having to sleep in his seat. Halfway through the journey, he'd been removed to the segregated car where, according to the conductor, there weren't any available sleeping berths. He'd seen several empty ones and realized what the man meant was that there weren't any available for folks that looked like him.

"Miles?"

He turned at the sound of a man's voice behind him. "Uncle Louis." He hadn't seen him in almost two years, but he'd recognize the big burly man anywhere. He was his father's youngest brother and the two favored each other.

His uncle pulled him into a spine-crushing hug. "You looking good, boy."

"Thanks. How's Mama?"

He shook his head. "Not good. That's why I'm glad you're here. Buggy's parked over there." Uncle Louis pointed. "She got sick about three weeks ago. She thought it was a little cold. We all did. She went to the doctor and he gave her some medicine. She started feeling better, then she was laid low again four days ago. Doctor said it's pneumonia. But it doesn't look good."

127

After being accustomed to driving, the slow pace of the horses threatened to send Miles around the bend. He needed to see Mama for himself. It took forty-five minutes to reach the farm. He saw rows and rows of vegetables planted and a few cattle roaming.

As soon as the buggy stopped, Miles hopped down, grabbed his bags and went inside. He set everything down, removed his hat and coat and hung them on the peg near the door. He inhaled the familiar lemon fragrance that Mama swore made everything extra clean and fresh and made his way to where he knew her bedroom to be. He heard the coughing before he reached the hallway. He tapped on the door.

"Miles." His Aunt Mae wrapped her thin arms around him. "She's been waiting for you." She stood off to the side.

He approached the bed and hunkered down on the side. "Hey, Mama. How's my best girl?" Her usually vibrant golden skin looked pale and she'd lost weight.

Her eyes opened and she rolled her head in his direction. "I knew you'd come, baby boy."

"I wouldn't be anywhere else." Miles placed a soft kiss on her brow. He fought to keep his emotions in check. He couldn't handle seeing her this way — so frail and thin.

Mama lifted her hand and he grasped it. She scrutinized him. "You look different."

He chuckled. "I look the same. Maybe a few months older."

She attempted to smile. "No, baby. Different. Like you've finally found peace."

He bowed his head. How had she known?

"She must be special to capture your heart."

"She is, Mama. Her name is Leigh and I want to marry her."

Her light brown eyes went wide. "Marry?" She tried to sit up and it brought on another coughing fit.

His aunt rushed over with a glass of water. "Here, Mama. Sip slowly."

After a few sips, she pushed the glass away and lay back on the pillows.

Miles's concern increased. "Mama, why don't you get some rest? We'll talk later."

"No. I don't have much time left and there are some things I need to tell you. Mae, can you leave us alone for a bit?"

Clearly his aunt didn't want to leave, but the determined look on his grandmother's face left her no choice.

"I won't stay long," Miles told her. He waited until she closed the door. "What is it, Mama?"

"Look in the top drawer of my night table and get that blue box."

He did as asked. The fabric looked old and had faded in some spots. "What's inside?"

"Things your father wanted you to have. Letters he and your mother wrote to each other, a locket and your mother's wedding ring. Your father instructed me to give it you once you found that special girl. And it looks like you have. Go ahead and open it."

He sat in the chair near her bed, undid the latch and surveyed the contents. He picked up the locket. A little polish would make it shine again. Inside was a photo of his mother on one side and his father on the other. He replaced it and opened the small ring box. The gold ring had a sapphire surrounded by diamonds in the center and a small round diamond on either side. He couldn't wait to see it on Leigh's finger. Mama had always said it would take an exceptional woman to settle his restless feet. She was right. Miles closed the box. He decided he'd read the letters later.

"Promise me you'll be happy, Miles."

"I am happy, Mama. I love you."

"Love you too, baby," she said softly.

He opened his mouth to ask her another question, but she had fallen asleep.

He leaned back and watched her. He had no idea he'd drifted off until a hand on his arm startled him.

Aunt Mae rubbed his shoulder. "Miles, dinner is on the stove. Get you something to eat and go rest. If I need you, I'll let you know."

Miles pushed to his feet. "Okay." He went to the bedroom he always used when he visited and cleaned up, then sat down to a meal of ham, beans, rice and cornbread. With his stomach full, it only took a few minutes for him to fall into a deep sleep.

His uncle woke him a few minutes before midnight. "Mama's gone."

He scrambled out of the bed, hastily dressed and ran into the room. He laid a palm on his grandmother's face. "Rest well, Mama." With his heart breaking, he clung to his aunt as they both sobbed out their grief. He thought about the promise he'd made earlier. He would be happy as soon as he got back to Leigh.

CHAPTER 12

Leigh and Liz were still laughing when they got to their apartments. "Messing around with you, I barely have time to get ready for tonight."

Liz looked contrite. "I know and I'm sorry. Who knew trying to find a dress would be that difficult." Mack had invited her to dinner. "Don't worry about cooking. Just come down and I'll have Victor fix you something. He'll bring it to the dressing room."

"That would be great." Leigh told her what she wanted. "Just a small portion. I don't want to be too full."

"Okay."

She went straight to the bathroom and started the water in the tub. While it ran, she laid her dress on the bed. She hadn't heard from Miles and had hoped to talk to him about the Paris invitation before the show. She'd told Liz about it and Liz said she should take advantage of it. But Leigh was hesitant to be so far from everything and everyone she knew. She couldn't even speak French, for heaven's sake. Putting it out of her mind, she got ready and went downstairs.

After consuming her dinner, she went in search of Miles. He would usually be here by now. She asked the band members and they hadn't seen him. Had something happened to him? Her fear mounted as the minutes ticked off. She asked some of the wait staff, as well as the two bouncers, but none of them had seen him.

"Belinda, have you seen Miles?"

"As a matter of fact I have. He stopped in earlier and asked me to give you this." Belinda pulled a folded slip of paper out of her pocket. "He was in a big hurry, had a suitcase in the car."

Leigh read the note: *Leigh, I have to leave. Sorry. Miles* "Did he say anything else?"

"No."

She swore the woman smiled. She read the note again. It didn't make sense. He told her he wasn't leaving, promised her. Fighting back tears, she went over to the stage to talk to her bandmates and called Liz over. They couldn't cancel, but they didn't have a piano player, either. Leigh didn't understand. She thought he'd changed.

Leigh barely got through the show. More than once, she glanced over to where Miles usually sat and kept expecting to hear his distinctive piano sound and his strong baritone. Later, in her room, she let the tears she'd been holding back come full force. She spent a restless night speculating on the whys. The next morning, she walked over to his apartment, only to be told that he was gone.

Liz came over. "Anything?"

"Nothing. I don't understand. He promised he was here to stay. Where could he have gone?" She'd imagined every scenario, but not one explained this. "Have you found someone to sit in at the piano?"

"Mack called in a favor. Says the guy is pretty good. Not as good as Miles, but he won't embarrass himself. Have you thought anymore about Paris?"

She groaned. "No."

"Well, you should."

"We'll see." Right now she couldn't concentrate on anything.

By Friday, Leigh made up her mind to travel to Paris. She needed the time away to clear her mind. And her heart. She'd purchased her ticket on the steamship and would leave tomorrow afternoon. Liz had found someone else to take her place for the month and she would start tonight, giving Leigh the time needed to take care of last-minute details.

She added more clothes to her suitcase. Tears threatened, but she refused to cry anymore. Willing them away, she continued the task of packing. As she emptied the next drawer, her gaze went to the sculpture sitting on the dresser. Her emotions welled once more. Despite everything, she couldn't leave it behind. Leigh repackaged it and wrapped it in one of her skirts for extra protection before placing it in the bag. It took her only a few minutes to finish. She glanced around at the room to make sure she had all she planned to take. She had some apprehension of what life would be like in Paris for the next month and how she would survive with the language barrier, but she was determined to forge ahead on this new adventure.

Leigh said the words confidently, however, when it came time to leave on Saturday, her fear and anxiety had risen to a level that made her consider canceling. Her gaze fixed on the large ship that would take her away.

"Liz, maybe this isn't such a good idea."

Her friend smiled understandingly. "It's a good idea, Leigh. What happened to that twenty-one year-old woman who hopped on a train to follow her dreams?" Liz grasped Leigh's hand. "You're going to be fine. Promise you'll write and tell me about all the fabulous places you've gone. Who knows, maybe I'll come visit."

She brightened. "That would be wonderful." She saw passengers starting to board. Though the ship wouldn't depart for another two hours, Leigh wanted to get there early enough to find her way around. She gave Liz a strong hug.

"Take care of yourself," Liz said thickly.

Leigh joined the line of passengers. She turned back and waved to Liz. The ship was even larger than she realized. She wandered through the huge space and found a smoking room and dining saloon. She returned above deck and stood against the rail looking out over the water. Though she'd never admit it aloud, she had still held out hope that Miles would show up. A searing pain tore through her heart. Never again.

* * *

Saturday, a travel-weary Miles stepped down from the train and walked to the parking area. He'd been in such a hurry to leave that he hadn't considered that his car might have been stolen. Thankfully, it sat parked right where he left it. They'd buried Mama on Thursday and he'd taken the first train out on Friday to get back. He probably should have gone home first to clean up and rest, but his fatigue took a back seat to seeing Leigh.

His knock went unanswered and he walked down and around to the restaurant. "Hey, Liz."

"Miles."

The frost in her voice and eyes confused him. "Is Leigh around?"

"Why do you care? It's obvious you had other plans."

"What are you talking about? I left her a note explaining where I'd gone."

"Oh, that *I have to leave, sorry* note."

His heart started pounding. "Liz, that is not what my note said. I had to leave to see about my grandmother."

"What did you say?"

"My grandmother was sick. I left the note with Belinda."

"Oh, no."

"Liz. What does that mean?" Instead of answering, she left him standing at the bar and went into the back. A moment later, she came back with Belinda. Belinda's eyes widened with fear when she saw Miles, alarming him. "Would someone tell me what's going on? Where is Leigh?"

"The note Leigh had only said that you were leaving," Liz confessed.

Miles turned a blazing stare at Belinda. "What did you do?" he shouted.

The fear in her eyes grew. "I...I..."

Liz looked stricken. "Leigh thought you'd left. We just dropped her off at the dock. She's on her way to Paris for a month."

He thought he might be sick. "What time does the ship leave?"

"Four."

He checked his watch. He had an hour and a half. Had he been the woman-beating type, he would have strangled Belinda.

"I'm sorry," Belinda cried.

Liz placed a hand on her hip. "Yes, you are. And you're fired. Collect your things and get out!"

"Liz, do you know how to drive?"

"No, but Anthony does." Anthony was one of the cooks.

"Have him meet me out front in fifteen minutes."

"Where are you going?"

"To pay my rent for the next month and then I'm going to get my woman." Miles strode out of the restaurant. He accomplished what he needed to do and was back in nine and a half minutes. The first copy of "Love's Serenade" had been waiting with his mail and he'd stuck it in his bag, but he couldn't even be happy about it. Not yet. Anthony was

135

waiting and Miles drove straight to the docks. He grabbed his suitcase and satchel out of the back seat and slapped the car key in Anthony's hand. "Take care of my car until I get back."

"Yes, sir."

"And Anthony, it better be in one piece."

"It will be, sir. I promise."

Miles hurried over to the ticket agent and prayed he'd still be able to purchase passage. There were a few people ahead of him and he anxiously willed them to hurry up. *Finally!* He walked up to the booth, paid the steep price quoted and boarded. There had to be a few hundred people milling about. How was he going to find Leigh? He saw few members of the race. In his haste, Miles nearly bowled over a man coming around a corner.

"My apologies, sir." He took in the man's attire and noticed he carried a Bible in his hand. He had kind blue eyes.

"No harm done. You seem to be in quite a hurry."

"Yes. I'm looking for someone." Something in the man's demeanor had Miles sharing his story of visiting his grandmother and Belinda's deceit.

"Sounds like you love this woman very much."

"I do. I had planned to ask her to marry me."

The man chuckled. "Well, if you find her, I'd be happy to do the honors. I'm traveling to Paris for missionary work. By the way, I'm Rev. Parks."

Miles thought that a splendid idea. "Miles Cooper. It's nice to meet you. How will I find you?"

"How about we meet over by that rail in, say, two hours. If you've found her and she's agreeable, we'll conduct the ceremony."

"And if I don't find her?"

He shrugged. "We try again tomorrow. You have a good six or seven days to make your case."

Miles found he liked the friendly minister. "Thank you."

"Godspeed."

He continued his search and had just about given up when he spotted Leigh leaning against the railing. His heart rate kicked up. He wove his way through the throng of people until he stood at her side. "Leigh."

"What are you doing here, Miles?" Leigh asked coldly.

It was the same question she'd asked almost three months ago at The Magnolia. "Did you actually think I'd leave you?"

"Oh, your note said everything. I think it would be best if we just moved on. I'm not going to keep—"

Miles silenced her tirade with a kiss. "My grandmother passed away."

She gasped softly. "What? I'm so sorry."

"Baby, the note Belinda gave you was not the one I wrote. My note said that I had to go see about my grandmother because she was sick and that I'd be back in a week or so."

"She…"

"Yes. I'm so sorry, Leigh. I wanted to wait for you, but I had to get to her."

Leigh faced the water and said nothing.

He plowed on with his explanation and she still never looked his way. Had he lost her for good? "Leigh, please say something."

"All the things I said about you, thought about you. I feel like such a fool."

Miles turned her face toward his. "You're not. She deceived you. I'm not leaving you, sweetheart. Ever." He touched his mouth to hers. "Ever."

"I don't want you to."

"Good. I love you, Leigh and I want to marry you."

Leigh's mouth dropped. "Say that again."

He grinned. "I love you and I want to marry you. Will you marry me?"

"Yes," she shouted.

He kissed her soundly, picked her up and swung her around. He set her gently on her feet and took her by the hand. "Come on."

Leigh laughed. "Where are we going?"

"To get married."

"Wait! What?" She stopped walking. "We can't get married. I need a dress, we have to make plans, we're going to be on this ship for almost a week."

"Yes, we can. And you look beautiful." She had on a lovely gray traveling suit. "We can have a big party or whatever you want when we get back home, but I don't want to wait another minute to have you as my wife."

She studied his face seemingly searching for some hint of guile. Finally, she nodded. "Okay. But how are we going to get married? Don't we need a minister?"

"I've got one," he said, hurrying to where he and Rev. Parks were supposed to meet.

"Miles Cooper, you'd better not be pulling my leg."

He chuckled. "I'm not." He spied Rev. Parks a few feet ahead.

Rev. Parks stood waiting at the designated spot with a broad smile. "Ah, I see you found her. The Lord answers prayers."

Yes, He did. "Rev. Parks, this is Leigh Jones."

"It's nice to meet you. It seems you and Miles share quite a history."

"It's nice to meet you, as well." Leigh smiled up at Miles. "Yes, we do."

"He said he wants to marry you. Are you agreeable?"

"Yes."

Rev. Parks opened his Bible.

Leigh stared. "Just like that?"

His robust laughter filled the air. "Unless, there's something else you need. I took the liberty of inviting a few of my missionary brothers and sisters to stand witness. I hope you don't mind."

Miles met the faces of the six people gathered and nodded a greeting, which they returned. "Not at all."

"Then, if we're ready."

He looked down at Leigh. "Ready, sweetheart?"

"Ready."

They repeated their vows and when it came time for the ring, Miles extracted his mother's ring from the small jewelers box and slid it onto Leigh's finger. "This belonged to my mother."

"Oh, Miles. It's beautiful."

Rev. Parks smiled. "I now pronounce you husband and wife. Miles, you may kiss your bride."

Miles didn't need any prompting. "You are my heart, Leigh." Mindful of their audience, he gave her a short, but sweet kiss. "We'll save the rest for later," he whispered. He shook the minister's hand and, after a few congratulatory remarks, Rev. Parks and his group departed, leaving Leigh and Miles alone. "Well, how does it feel?"

"It feels wonderful, *amazing*. I still can't believe it." Leigh held up her hand and looked at the ring. "Are you sure your mother would approve?"

"My father left it for me to give to the woman who captured my heart. So, yes, he and my mother would approve."

"I love you so much."

"And I you." He gathered her in his embrace. He remembered the record. "I have something to show you." He reached into his satchel and took out the large envelope.

Leigh opened it. "Oh, my." She ran her hand over the label bearing their names. "It's real," she said emotionally. She held it against her. "We really did it."

"We did."

Smiling around her tears, she leaned up and kissed him.

"So, I hear you're going to be singing at some festivals. Would you by chance need a piano player?"

"I don't need just any piano player. I need you, Miles. Only you."

"Baby, you have me for the rest of our lives. Every day when the sun rises, your voice is the first thing on my mind. It's the music of my heart, a rare and precious find. A beautiful melody sung one note at a time, creating our own love's serenade," he sang softly to her. He pulled her closer and reveled in her nearness. He'd found the cure for his restless feet. He'd found love.

Dear Reader,

I am so excited to be part of this groundbreaking project. I'm a music lover, so it was an easy choice to set my story in this era. Leigh Jones and Miles Cooper come from different backgrounds, but they have one thing in common — music. It brought them together once and, with a little persistence on the part of Miles, it can, hopefully, do it again. But he has his work cut out for him. I had a ball bringing their story to life and hope you enjoy their journey to finding love again, while savoring a taste of the 1920s Harlem jazz scene.

Next month, look for The Art of Love (Decades: A Journey of African American Romance Book 4) by my author sister, Suzette Harrison.

As always, I so appreciate all your love and support. Without you, I couldn't do this. Let's keep in touch!

Much love,
Sheryl

Website: www.sheryllister.com
Email: sheryllister@gmail.com
Facebook: www.facebook.com/sheryllisterauthor/
Twitter: https://twitter.com/1Slynne

Acknowledgements

My Heavenly Father, thank you for my life. You never cease to amaze me with Your blessings!

To my husband Lance, you continue to show me why you'll always be my #1 hero!

To my children, family and friends thank for your continued support. I appreciate and love you!

To Wayne Jordan, thank you for including me in this special project.

A special thank you to the readers and authors I've met on this journey. You continue to enrich my life.

A very special thank you to my agent, Sarah E. Younger and Natanya Wheeler, my personal miracle workers. I appreciate you more than words can say.

Advance Praise

"Sheryl Lister's *Love's Serenade* is a beautiful tribute to an era when men were gentlemen and ladies were women. You'll truly savor this step back in time, and becoming lost in a world of music and passion. The second chance at love that it serves is absolutely satisfying." — Suzette D. Harrison, Author of *Taffy* & *The Art of Love*

Discover More by Sheryl Lister
Contemporary Romance

Just To Be With You
All Of Me
It's Only You
Be Mine For Christmas (Unwrapping The Holidays Anthology)
Tender Kisses (The Grays of Los Angeles Book 1)
Places In My Heart (The Grays of Los Angeles Book 2)
Giving My All To You (The Grays of Los Angeles Book 3)
Embracing Forever (Book 3 in the ONCE UPON A BRIDESMAID Series) by Sheryl Lister
Made To Love You
It's You That I Need
Perfect Chemistry

Next in the Decades series:

Ava Lydell is chasing her dream. A gifted artist, she's fled the violence of the Deep South for the sunny seduction of California. As luck would have it, the economic crisis of The Great Depression interferes with her hopes and plans. Without patronage and reliable sales, her fledgling art studio fails. Now, she faces poverty, eviction...and the distraction of a mysterious, young stranger engaged in a questionable trade that delivers danger to Ava's front door.

In an age of Prohibition and poverty, Chase Jenkins has more than most Colored men. He's savvy, successful, and perilously employed. A bootlegger living on the wrong side of the law, he's determined to discover who murdered his baby brother. He has no time for diversions. Especially one packaged in the form of a "midnight" beauty with sultry lips and curvaceous hips. Unable to deny her allure, he involves himself in her affairs despite better judgment. What begins as a crisis quickly becomes a risky romance. Join Chase and Ava on their journey as they survive danger only to indulge in the art of love.

About the Author

Sheryl Lister is a multi-award winning author who has enjoyed reading and writing for as long as she can remember. After putting writing on the back burner for several years, she became serious about her craft in 2009. When she's not reading or writing, Sheryl can be found on a date with her husband or in the kitchen creating appetizers and bite-sized desserts. Sheryl resides in California and is a wife, mother of three and former pediatric occupational therapist. She is a member of RWA, CIMRWA, the Kiss of Death Chapter of RWA, and is represented by Sarah E. Younger of Nancy Yost Literary Agency.

CPSIA information can be obtained
at www.ICGtesting.com
Printed in the USA
LVHW02s1545200418
574265LV00009B/365/P